# Black Eye

*A Make You Mine Romance*

KIMBERLEY ANNE

Cover design by Judith San Nicolas
Typeset in Avenir Next LT Pro 26pt/Centaur 11pt
Printed and bound in Australia by IngramSpark
Prepared for publication and edited by Dr Juliette Lachemeier @ The Erudite Pen: theeruditepen.com

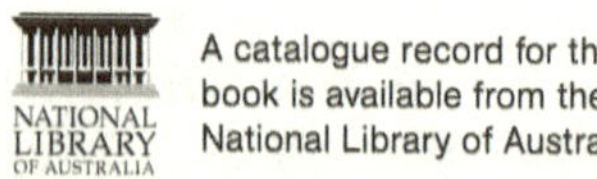
A catalogue record for this book is available from the National Library of Australia

**Black Eye: A Make You Mine Romance - Book Two in the Acoustic Series**
First ed.
ISBN  9780645784527
E-ISBN  9780645784534

To my family ♥ Thank you for daring me to dream and allowing me to inspire you with yours.

To my readers ♥ Without you none of this would be possible.

# A Make You Mine
# Romance

Book Two

# Acoustic Novel Series

# Prologue

*Morgan Campbell, April 2018*

'Mac!' Morgan Campbell's brother yelled.

Morgan cringed.

She hated that nickname, the initials of the name given to her at birth, Morgan Asher Campbell, especially when he yelled it at her.

She knew by the tone of his voice exactly what he wanted. And it wasn't what she wanted.

Lucas Campbell was her brother, five years older than Morgan's twenty-five years. He had shown up at her house in Mulwala, a country town on the New South Wales border to Victoria. Morgan had been living here happily for twelve months by herself before Lucas had invited himself, telling his younger sister that he needed a place to stay for a couple of weeks. That was twelve months ago. Morgan had tried numerous times of late to kick him out, each time unsuccessful. Every time she told Lucas he had to move on, she found him sitting in her lounge room when she got home from work.

'Morgan.' Lucas yelled her Christian name to get her attention. He was closer to her bedroom door this time. Next, he would bang on her door, until she answered him, or she opened her door to glare at him. Morgan's bedroom door was locked. Lucas wasn't allowed in her room ever. But that didn't stop him from trying.

Trying to ignore her brother, he hoped that he would take her non-response as a hint that she didn't want to go out tonight. But he yelled her name again.

Morgan stood from her bed, preparing for her class tomorrow. She was a primary school teacher, teaching the third grade.

Her hand reached the door handle as his fist hit the wood of her door. She felt the woosh of air surround her as she turned the handle and pulled back. She glared at Lucas, knowing he was in a mood and wasn't going to leave her alone.

Morgan felt her arm leave her side, then her body was moving. Lucas had pulled his sister forcefully away from her comfort zone, which was her bedroom. He had a hold of her forearm, and she could feel his hand tightening. He was angry she had ignored him.

'We're leaving.' Lucas had turned toward the front door taking his sister with him. Luckily, Morgan was already dressed in jeans, a tee-shirt and boots, not in her pyjamas and slippers, for when her brother was moody like this.

There was no point in arguing with him when he was like this. She did herself no favours by opening her mouth. It only made Lucas see red, and when he saw red, as she had learnt over the last six months, everything she owned copped it.

# Black Eye

His abuse towards her was getting worse, hence the reason her bedroom door was locked, and she was behind it. If there was one thing her brother had taught her over the time that he had been living with her, it was that she had to think quickly and always remember to lock her door and have her bedroom keys in her pocket. With her bedroom door still in reach, all Morgan had to do was pull it closed. A brief feeling of relief washed over her every time she heard the lock click into place.

Morgan told herself she was safe behind her locked door, and that Lucas couldn't hurt her. He couldn't throw her furniture at her or the little knick-knacks she had purchased to make this little house she rented from the education department a home. There wasn't much left that Lucas hadn't broken and this made her wonder what would happen when there was nothing left to ruin. Would he barge through her bedroom door and start throwing what she had managed to save since she'd become a teacher three years ago? Would her brother destroy everything that she had worked so hard for over the last two years since she moved here until there was absolutely nothing left? Then would she be the only punching bag he had?

There had to be a way out from under her brother's thumb. His behaviour was only getting worse. His abuse had started with a grab of her arm here and a punch to her upper arm there. Most of the time, Morgan tried to avoid him and hang around work longer to stay out of his way. When Lucas cottoned on that she was spending less and less time around him, his behaviour became more aggressive.

'Lucas.' It came out softly as not to aggravate her brother further, and when she tugged her arm backwards, he let go. 'I can make my own way to the car.'

She told herself that it was easier to do what Lucas wanted to do rather than fight him. Maybe tonight would be the night that changed everything. Morgan could only hope.

Lucas snatched the keys from the kitchen bench and headed towards the front door.

She stumbled across the threshold between inside and out because he pushed her through the front door and quickly slammed it. Morgan moved towards the passenger seat. There was no way Lucas was going to let her drive, even if the car was hers. As Lucas had taken to driving her car everywhere, that left Morgan with no mode of transportation. With her money already scarce as she paid all the bills and he contributed to nothing, she couldn't afford to purchase another vehicle. The only other option she could afford was a second-hand bicycle.

Lucas unlocked the car, and they both got in. Five minutes later, he parked outside The Grand Hotel, the local pub in this country town that attracted the attention of the roughest people, Lucas's type of people. Morgan hated coming to the front bar.

Her brother walked closely next to her as maybe he thought she would run from him. The thought did cross her mind. But the feeling that started to grow inside her was like adrenaline running through her veins. It told her there was a chance that tonight might turn out better than she thought it would.

As soon as they walked through the doors of the front bar, she cringed inwardly, hoping it wouldn't show on the outside. On an exhale, she breathed out her relief. Lucas' attention had been drawn away from her. He was now moving towards his newfound friends – the ones he had made since moving in with her. Morgan followed behind him, as that was what was expected of her. Her brother would drink and converse vulgarly with his creepy friends while she sat in silence, waiting for her brother to be done drinking and wanting her to drive him home.

Lucas always encouraged her to drink with him, but she refused. She wanted to be in control and didn't want anyone to take advantage of her. Watching the amount of alcohol he drank turned Morgan off drinking altogether. They had only been there an hour, and he had poured more than two jugs of beers down his throat. But Morgan wasn't thinking about trying to escape Lucas and his friends. Someone new had just walked in. He was tall and lean and didn't look like he was from around here. But the familiarity worn on his dark features told her he knew about this pub, or at least places like this. He was the perfect guy for Morgan to fantasise about.

No one new ever walked into the front bar of The Grand Hotel. She should know. She was here often enough with Lucas. The people here were all locals. But when the door opened an air of freshness walked in, Morgan knew in that moment that things here at this bar were about to change.

She was the only person who noticed him walk in. Everyone else was too busy laughing or shouting or cosying up to their other halves. His brown eyes caught her hazel eyes, but that wasn't the only thing that caught, so had her intake of air. She must've looked like she was prey in the spotlight. Why was she wondering what he was thinking about the look on her face? And why was she thinking this man could be the answer to her shitty situation? Why was she even fantasising about him?

Her situation wasn't changing tonight, it seemed. He broke eye contact first to continue to walk straight up to the bar, find a stool and order his drink. A tumbler with brown liquor at the bottom, no ice. The mystery air of freshness might have ordered his drink, but it didn't stop him from checking out the crowd that had gathered tonight at The Grand Hotel. It was rowdier in here than usual.

Their eyes met a few times before they both looked away. He was checking her out, the same as she was checking him out. Morgan liked the attention she was getting from him. Even if she didn't know this man, his eyes on her never creeped her out once, unlike when Lucas's friends looked at her. Her skin crawled every time.

She watched on as the brown liquor was gone in one swallow, before the tumbler was slammed back down on top of the bar. *Someone was in a mood,* Morgan thought. He ordered another, but he didn't drink this one the same way. His drink made it to his lips a few times before he returned it to the bar.

'Order a drink, we're getting drunk.' Her brother had come up behind her.

'No. You are drinking. I am just the ride home.' Lucas was making a scene. Morgan was having none of it.

'Come on, loosen up a bit. Let me order you a drink.'

'I said no.' Her words came out at the top of her lungs.

Stepping back from the high-top table, Lucas and his friends had gathered around to avoid him pulling her back in and taking a hold of her forearm, where he would most likely give her a Chinese burn for making a scene in front of his friends.

Morgan took off at a pace, slowing only when she passed the man seated at the bar, he had picked up his drink and swallowed it just as she stopped in front of him. Pissed off at her brother and now that she was closer to him, she was pissed at this gorgeous stranger. He had been checking her out for as long as he'd been here and didn't once try to make a move. He could have been her knight in shining armour, but all he wanted to do was drink, just like her brother.

Blowing out a frustrated breath through parted lips before Morgan pressed them in a thin line, shook her head in displeasure and stormed out of the front bar through the doors that would lead her to the back bar and the bistro.

Angry at her brother and everything that had happened since he moved in with her, Morgan let her emotions get the better of her. Now, she was hiding in the employee-only area hoping she wasn't followed.

Under the stairs in the darkness, Morgan let the tears that had welled in her eyes fall down her cheeks. She let her frustrations out on a silent scream, which must have looked ridiculous to the person watching at her. Jarryd Thomas, the middle child of Jackie Thomas, the owner of this establishment, was staring right at her with his hand out. He gave her the come-here gesture. On a whim, knowing that her night wasn't going to get any better, she took his hand and let him lead her out from underneath the stairs and then up them.

Once out of sight and earshot of everyone, Jarryd spoke. 'Ms Campbell.'

'You don't have to call me that.' Though she knew Jarryd was only being polite.

'Mac.'

Every person Morgan made contact with called her Mac, no thanks to her brother. She hated it. Wished everyone would call her Morgan. Maybe one day when her brother was out of her life, she could educate the people around her to use her Christian name.

'Why did you bring me up here, Jarryd?' She was curious as to why this Thomas brother had brought her up here.

'If it wasn't for your brother, I know you wouldn't even be downstairs in the front bar.'

Jarryd's observation was true. She wouldn't be here. She would be making notes for her grade three classes and marking their homework. Now, she would have to get up early tomorrow and get to work to do what she should be doing tonight.

Morgan nodded, and before she could say anything, Jarryd spoke again. 'No one uses the apartment up here. I think my mum wants my older brother Jaime to have it but seeing as he isn't around, maybe you could use it. Get away from your brother for a little while.'

'Jarryd, the thought is very sweet, but I can't just stay here without your mum knowing.'

'She doesn't come up here, and I'll give you a key. Let yourself in or come in before closing if you don't want to use the key.'

What did Morgan say to the first opportunity she'd been given since her brother had arrived a year ago to be able to have a break from him? She knew if she played her cards right, she could do this. As sneaky as it would be, Morgan could avoid her brother to get the alone time she'd been missing out on.

She thanked Jarryd as he left her there in the apartment above The Grand Hotel. She didn't bother looking around, but headed straight for the king-size bed, crawled under the covers and fell asleep. She would worry about accepting Jarryd's offer another day.

# One

*Connor Black, May 2018*

'You're not the only one who can play the guitar, Zach. Lex and I know how to play, too. You could have at least stayed for the whole three songs. We just wanted to show our support. We didn't do it to piss you off.'

My sister Lex and I had surprised our brother Zach last night at his annual acoustic shindig.

Zach just stood at his front door and stared at me. His tone was sharp and not lost on me. 'Is there a reason why you've dragged my arse out of bed this early this morning? I really did want a sleep-in today. It's my day off, and I could use a quiet one.'

There was a moment's silence between us. I was here for a reason. I had to tell him what I'd done. I just didn't know how. So here went nothing.

'I sold them.' I let that information sink in. 'I sold every single one of them.' Another silence. 'Every single business I ever owned, dodgy and legit.'

Zach was the first person I'd asked when I needed capital for my business ventures, and at first, he'd been happy to help me out. But after seeing how ruthless I had become running my businesses, Zach had stopped offering business advice and opted to be a silent partner.

Now we were no longer business partners. I'd returned his capital and then some. My younger brother deserved the payout I gave him, especially given the shit I'd dragged him through with my ties to my less-than-legitimate businesses. He now didn't have to worry anymore about every way that I had fucked things up over the last ten years of my life.

'Connor. Are you serious?'

I knew the words I had spoken affected him, too. Harley, his girlfriend, had noticed, as she now stood by Zach's side. He was lucky to have someone he could hold on to.

'You're right. I am an arsehole.' I took a deep breath and tried to get my next words out, hoping that I didn't falter. 'To you, to Harley, to everyone – I'm sorry. My family deserves better from me. I want to be better.'

There was another silence as I turned my attention towards Harley. 'I didn't know you were my brother's woman.' I stared at the female in front of me, and she looked up at Zach. It seemed she didn't know she was his woman, either.

I was sure those two could work that one out, so I continued, not breaking eye contact with Harley. 'Your family moved in next door after I moved to Melbourne. I didn't know you then and didn't know you and Zach were close. You were going to be my ticket, Harley. You and I, we could have been so rich.

But I only ever thought about myself and no one else. I'm sorry for every arsehole thing I've ever done to you and my brother.'

I didn't wait for a response from Zach or Harley. 'I know I deserved the punch you gave me,' I confessed. 'For what I'd done to you over the years, and for not considering Harley's needs about a music career. It was the wake-up call I needed. I don't want to be that man. I sold everything for a clean slate.' I didn't know why, but my confession felt right. I owed Zach that much.

There was another silence between the three of us, and I really needed to get out of here. 'Lex let me borrow her car to come here. I'd better make a move so she can head back to Melbourne. Thanks for the chance to apologise. Sorry I interrupted your personal time.'

'You're not going back with Lex?'

'No.' I shook my head. 'If I want my clean slate to work, I need to stay away from temptation, and Melbourne is full of it.'

'Connor, if you're serious about your clean slate, don't be a stranger.' Zach shoved his hand in my direction, and accepting his offer, we shook hands. 'If you're done being a dick, it would be nice to have my big brother back.'

My apology would go a long way to mend the burnt bridges of our relationship. Afterall, I was the one who'd moved to Melbourne to complete my business degree. I couldn't begrudge the relationship I had with my younger brother. It had been his choice to stay in the serenity of the town we grew up in to build his name in the hospitality industry and make himself an upstanding member of Mulwala.

I heard the front door close behind me as I made my way over to our sister Lex's black Commodore and got myself the hell out of there. Zach lived by the river and was more than a few minutes out of town. I guessed he liked the quietness of it all.

I started the car Lex had let me borrow to make my apology and let my thoughts drift to all the moments my younger sister and I had spent together in Melbourne, catching up for coffee, dinner and to play guitar. Lex, like me, had also decided to move to Melbourne after high school to complete her accounting degree. She had let me ride along yesterday on her trip up from Melbourne. But as Harley had tagged along too, I just laid on the backseat and remained silent the whole way. I didn't mind, really. It gave me a chance to lull myself into the rumble of the V8 and catch up on some much-needed shut-eye.

The V8 rumbled under the hood again as I put the car in gear. The sound had become magic to my ears. One I never thought I would like. I no longer had a car as I had sold that too. It was tied up with my businesses, so I'd had to let my Subaru BRZ go. Maybe I was wrong to decide not to have a car. Maybe I just needed one with a rumble like this.

I guided my sister's lowered Commodore gently over the dirt road as I made my way back towards the house I grew up in. The house my sister had purchased from my parents when they'd decided to move to Melbourne to chase their professional dreams. Just the same as two of their three children had done. Once I hit the bitumen, I moved quickly through the gears to top speed. I felt the rush in my veins as the car moved like a Supercar. Fast. I slowed down as I reached civilisation. I didn't want to get caught by the cops. I was still an arsehole, but it was a work in progress not to be.

I pulled the Commodore into my sister's drive. I didn't even have the chance to get out before I saw Lex had taken one step away from her front door. She stood on her front step with her hand on her hip. She was just like our mother, a trained psychologist, but I'd never tell her that. Lex pried for information the same way our mother did.

'How did it go?'

She knew I'd needed to see Zach, but she didn't know the reason. She would know soon enough when I didn't return to Melbourne with her. 'He wasn't happy I dragged his arse out of bed.'

Lex scoffed at me. 'What did you expect? He hadn't seen Harley in four weeks, so he'd probably had her up all night.'

'Lex, that's too much information.' It wasn't an image I wanted inside my head. I brushed passed her and into the family home she'd decided she wanted to hold onto as her own. Lex had told everyone in our family that she couldn't stand the thought of someone else living in her childhood home. But it was more than that – this house was our family's sanctuary and if Lex wasn't unwinding here, then the rest of us were allowed to.

'So, things are okay between you two then?' Like a dog with a bone, she wouldn't let this go.

'Alex,' I cut her off, making my way to the kitchen to grab a bottle of water. I drank it all in one go as I leaned up against the kitchen bench.

Lex gave me a look that told me she wouldn't take my shit. I think she enjoyed every chance she got to put me in my place, even though she was six years younger than me. I wouldn't ever admit I needed her in my life to help me keep my shit together.

'Alex, it was one conversation. There's still a long way to go before Zach and I are friends again.' There was a gentleness in my voice. She didn't need me to piss her off.

'Well, don't be an arsehole all the time then,' she threw back at me and lightly punched my shoulder.

'Easier said than done.'

'Work on it. Are you ready to make a move back to Melbourne?'

Here went nothing. 'Sorry, sis. You're on your own for the trip back.'

'What have you done, Connor?' Lex's mouth hung open as she stared at me.

'It's not what you think, Lex.' But my words don't convince her.

'Are you in trouble? Why would you want to stay here?' The confusion on her face was cute. If she knew, I thought that she would find a way to hurt me. Use her martial arts to take me down.

'Alex,' I clipped her name to get her attention. 'I'm not in trouble, I just don't want to go back to Melbourne.'

'What the fuck? Connor!' My sister almost shouted at me. Two older brothers gifted her with how to swear like a trooper.

Soft words then left Lex's potty mouth. 'Talk to me.'

There was a silence between us as we glared at each other. Lex regained her composure, then got in my face. 'You better sit the fuck down on the lounge and tell me everything now.' Her long finger pressed into my chest bone.

I guess the apple didn't fall far from the tree, with my sister's ability to psycho-analyse. Lex had picked up a few tricks from our mum. I wasn't sure where I should start. With everything that had happened recently, I just knew I needed to tell my sister all of it. If I didn't, she wouldn't rest until she had every last detail.

'I sold everything.' I surprised my sister just like I had Zach. I let that information sink in. Once I knew she understood, I continued. 'I sold all my businesses. Even the car and apartment had to go.'

Lex looked intently at me with her mouth wide open again, taking a moment to think things over. 'Oh my God, Connor. Why?'

'Truthfully, after I lucked out with the offer I made to Harley James, I didn't see the point anymore.' It was half the truth. The brunette at The Grand that had caught my eye four weeks ago was the other half of the truth, but I didn't tell Lex any of that. 'When Zach punched me for manhandling Harley, it was a wakeup call. One I needed. I don't want to be that man anymore.'

'Now what?' Lex was always concerned about me. Was it because of our shared experience living in Melbourne? Did she ever worry about Zach like she did me, because he was here in Mulwala and not Melbourne? Or was it because of my ruthless tendencies and the man I had become, and that Zach was the polar opposite to me?

'Not sure,' I told my sister honestly. 'There's nothing left in Melbourne for me anymore. Thought I might stay here and try to figure a few things out.'

'Clean slate, hey?' Lex's eyebrow was raised. The Black family trademark: one raised eyebrow.

'Something like that.' I didn't really know. What I did know was that if I ran into one hazel-eyed brunette, I would find a way to hold on to her and not let her go.

Lex got up from the lounge and kissed my check. 'Stay as long as you like. Just don't trash the place, and keep working on things with Zach.' She reached for her bags, then stopped. 'What about the money, Connor?'

Lex's question caught me off guard. She was always the accountant. I hadn't thought about the money I had made from the sale of my businesses or the debt I no longer had, and I didn't want to think about it right now. I needed a break before I dealt with my money. I didn't know what I was going to do next, but I knew I needed to figure a few things out and make a plan.

'Lex, leave the money alone. Don't look into it. Don't touch it. Any of it.' I grabbed her hand and squeezed it to reinforce my point. 'Alex.' I used her given name on purpose. 'This is important. Leave. The. Money. Alone. There are things I need to deal with first, then the money is all yours to look after. Okay!'

'Okay!' Lex grabbed her bags and headed for the front door. She was grumpy. I'd called her Alex. My sister had decided, at some point in her life, that she didn't want to be called Alex. She insisted everyone call her Lex.

I tried the gentle approach. 'Lex, I mean it.'

'I said okay, Connor.' My sister had reigned in her sass the tiniest amount for me.

I followed her out the front door and watched as she put her bags and guitar in the boot of her car. I would reach out to Zach when I was ready. Maybe Lex knew he wasn't high on my priority list of people I wanted to interact with. I waved goodbye as she pulled out of her drive to make her way back to Melbourne.

# Two

Closing the front door, I headed to the lounge to sit down when I heard the familiar sound that was my ringtone. As my phone vibrated on the surface of the kitchen bench, I debated whether or not I should answer. Picking up my phone, I saw who was calling. I tossed it back onto the bench.

It was my lawyer, the one I had recently told to take a hike. He was an even bigger son of a bitch than me. Always after the next big dollar, and I was his ticket. That was because I'd thought Harley was my ticket. At least now that I was attempting to work on a clean slate, I wouldn't chase the next big dollar. And the type of people I wanted in my circle of acquaintances would be different.

I wasn't in the business of favours anymore. I had sold practically everything, paid my debts, and I didn't owe anyone. Anything. Anymore. And no one needed to know where the fuck I was. Maybe I was more serious about this clean slate than

I'd led myself to believe. Could this small town and the woman I wanted to see again have had that much of an effect on me? I wasn't sure, but I wanted to find out. I wanted to follow that road and see where it would take me.

So, I picked up the set of house keys Lex had left me and pocketed them, leaving my phone on the bench. I wouldn't need that for the rest of the day, and it would be nice not to have the damn thing attached to me. I locked the front door and headed for the one place that served the one thing I needed.

I walked the distance from Lex's house on the Murray River to The Grand Hotel that sat on the corner of Melbourne Road and Bayly Street. The two-kilometre walk helped the smallest amount to clear my head, but I was in need of a drink. I was crazy to think a hazel-eyed brunette would be at the pub at this time of day, but I was out of sorts and in a mood, and I needed to let what I was feeling go. Melbourne didn't need me any more than I needed it. I wasn't tied to the city or the acquaintances I'd had business dealings with. No one I associated with needed me, including the lawyer that had been under my employ.

I opened the door and was instantly assaulted by the commotion. It was the middle of the morning. Voices grunted and yelled. It was true this place was totally feral, but I just didn't think it would be at this time of the day. It was loud and all I wanted was a quiet beer. I took in the scene before me and wondered if I should bother, when I saw the look on the face of the skinny-arse kid behind the bar. I didn't hesitate and moved closer to the loud voices.

'Take it outside. There's a smoker's area for your bullshit,' I said evenly in the direction of the raised voices.

Heads turned to face me. I wasn't scared. I would take them all on. Standing at just over six foot, the look on my face and the muscles that filled out my frame were usually enough to get people to walk away. Occasionally, there were idiots that wanted to take me on. Like today.

'Excuse me,' they both said. The rest of the pub had gone quiet as they waited to see what I would do.

Some people just needed shit spelled out. 'I said. Take. It. Out. Side.'

'Who are you to tell us what to do?'

'Someone who wants to enjoy a drink without the shit show.' I stared between the two guys who were making the most noise.

Both men scoffed, and I repeated myself again. 'Take it outside.' I wanted to scoff back at them but thought better and kept it to myself.

I watched both their arses leave, with their beers in tow, as I walked to the bar. I sat down on one of the unclaimed barstools. Silence followed as the door swung shut. Then conversation returned. The noise level was now bearable. My fingers tapped the wooden bar surface as I waited to be served. But it seemed some patrons were still stunned by my actions. Their eyes followed me. All I wanted was to taste beer on my tongue, let it slide down my throat and settle in my stomach.

'What does it take to get a drink around here?' I said to no one in particular. Then into the silence that had fallen over the pub once more. 'Please.'

It wasn't the skinny-arse bartender that moved towards me. It was a woman the same age as my mother who stepped in front of me. Her dyed chestnut hair was long and hung over her shoulders. Her tee-shirt wasn't too loose but not too tight either, and her legs filled out well-loved jeans. Pub life had worn on her, but you knew she was the boss.

'What can I get you?' Her face looked tired, and I wasn't sure how to read her expression. So, I didn't. I just asked for a drink. 'Beer, thanks.'

'Got a preference?' Her voice was slightly husky. Like she had yelled one too many times at idiots like those who had just left, that was my bet. But there was no sting in her timbre. Or maybe she just didn't bother anymore. A paying customer was a paying customer. Right.

'As long as it's cold and not from the tap.' I knew sometimes the tap lines weren't always clean.

I was handed a bottle with the lid popped off. I turned the bottle around and read the label. James Squire. I brought the bottle to my lips, sipped and swallowed. Then held out my card to pay.

When no one reached to take my payment, I said, 'What do I owe you?'

'It's on the house for those two,' the woman explained, nodding her head in the direction of the two idiots who had just left. 'I just can't seem to get them to leave anymore,' she added, her eyebrows knitting together, like maybe she didn't want me to know that piece of information.

'Need me to hang around more often then?' The words slipped out of my cocky mouth before I knew what I'd done. I brought my beer to my lips and took another sip. There were times I just shouldn't think. Or speak for that matter. It was how I got myself into trouble more times than not. But I thought this time, the trouble might actually be worth it. If a particular hazel-eyed brunette ever showed up.

When I didn't get an answer, I questioned what she had just told me. 'How often does this happen?'

'It's not your problem,' she threw back at me.

Maybe I should leave well enough alone. It really wasn't my problem. But what the hell? I didn't have anything else to do.

'So, it's a problem then?' I raised my family's trademark one eyebrow in a challenge and waited to see what the reaction would be.

'Argh,' slipped from her mouth, frustration evident as she rolled her eyes and dropped her hands to her hips.

I stayed silent, in hope that the void would be filled. I didn't have to wait too long.

'Those two are here all the time,' I heard two male voices say.

Then the younger voice, 'Though they are making a habit of coming in earlier and earlier. It's usually worse after five o'clock.'

So, it was a problem and not a little one, either.

# Three

I looked in the direction of the male voices. One stood behind the bar, the skinny-arse bartender, who couldn't have been much more than eighteen. The other sat on a barstool on the other side of the bar. They both looked at me, and I stared back at them. It was easy to see who these two belonged to – the woman in front of me. The boys shared the same features as their mother, lanky with chestnut hair and ocean blue eyes. Only the boy on the barstool was younger, not older than fifteen.

'Jarryd, Jason. I think I can handle this.' The woman in front of me turned to face her sons.

'Well maybe he can help, Mum?' Both sons eyed her with hope.

*Did I really want to help out though?* That was the question I had to ask myself. Did I want to jump straight back into the fire I had just gotten myself out of? Maybe it would be different this time. I couldn't just let savages overrun this pub, not when there were too many good memories here to let this go.

I had never before let my dick into the equation, but maybe I needed to start. I knew I needed to see her again, and this was where I saw her last. I would do anything to see the hazel-eyed brunette from that night four weeks ago and to know that she was a local.

The vision of her as she'd walked past me had not left me alone. The things I wanted to do to her played on my mind. I needed to feel what I'd felt that night as I sat on a stool in this bar. I had slammed back a shot of whiskey to drown out being thrown out of my brother's rooftop bar. My ruthless self was in a mood that night. It was why I had ended up here. But seeing her look at me the same way I was looking at her, the fiery anger I'd felt towards my brother Zach had burned out. It was replaced with a rush, a tingle of emotion that could have been love at first sight but was most likely lust.

For four weeks, I had held onto that feeling of lust. And for four weeks, I had wanted more of it. More of her. To hold on to her and that feeling I'd had inside. Hold on and not let either of them go: the tingles and the tiny sparks, feeling the rush run through my veins after my heart stopped momentarily then fluttered in its restart.

'Look at him, Mum,' the younger boy said. 'He just got those two to take it outside.'

'Where is Jaime? Have either of you heard from your brother?'

Maybe it had been their other brother's job to help out with the crowd that came in here?

Her boys just shrugged, and I guess that helped make up her mind.

I smirked. *Maybe this would be good for me,* I told myself. Maybe I needed to see how the other half lived. Bring my pedestal down a couple of notches before someone fly-kicked me off it and I landed too heavily on my arse.

'What do you know about country towns and a place like this?' Her head indicated the pub we were in. Her question halted my thoughts about the brunette and my past and brought me back into the present.

I didn't want to give away anything from my previous life. No one here in this town needed to know about the businesses I once owned and how I'd conducted said businesses. I might concede I lived here once. Someone was bound to figure that shit out anyway. This was my chance, though, to let the past go and only focus on my future.

But I needed to answer the question I had been asked. 'Word always travels fast in a country town, and as for places like this,' I lifted my chin to indicate the area that surrounded me, 'this not so much.' The words I spoke were the truth. Never before had I done hard labour. Mostly, I sat behind my desk and ran the show. Just like I assumed the woman in front of me did. The only difference being that she'd earned her way there. Me, not so much.

'Alright, well, I guess I have my work cut out for me then.' There was a small curve of her lips upwards. Thoughts ran through me, like the woman in front of me might just know how to bring pedestals down a few notches but also bring out the best in the people she hired.

I returned her small smile as I brought my beer to my lips and downed what was left. I just hoped what I had put my foot in didn't come back to boot me in the face or kick me in the teeth.

'Come on, let me show you around.' The smile I was just given wasn't shared with many, I could tell.

'Now?' I wanted to enjoy a few beers and then go back to my sister's to lie around for the rest of the day.

'You want the job. You start now.' She was the boss and not afraid to use her authority. I knew she would enjoy this, getting in my face and always telling me what to do. Maybe that was exactly what I needed for this clean slate of mine.

'So much for a few quiet beers,' I mumbled as I put my empty bottle down.

'Then you shouldn't have said anything.' The smirk thrown my way told me that this woman did know how to have some fun.

*Why did I have to say something?* God only knew why. I certainly didn't, that was for sure. I was a glutton for punishment, that much I did know. Maybe karma had found a way to catch up with me – this time. Maybe I needed her to make me a better person. Karma knew I wasn't a lost cause, though. She knew I needed to know that what went around came back around, and it needed to kick me firmly in the arse. To change my path. To send me in the right direction, a direction different to the one I had been travelling.

I pushed away from the bar and made my way over to where the older woman now stood next to her son at the back bar, then waited for her to start this show.

'I'm Jackie.' She held out her hand.

'Connor.' I took the hand she held out for me to shake.

'Let me show you around,' Jackie said, making small talk and pointing out the obvious as we toured around this small-town pub.

# Black Eye

There was a front bar that I had become familiar with since turning eighteen. It was this bar that attracted the after-five workers. There was a back bar that I hadn't been dragged into in a while, but knew it appealed to couples and families who came here to eat out in the bistro. There had been numerous interior renovations in the years I had been away. The back bar was bigger than the front bar, and there was enough room in here now to set up a small spot and get an individual or a duo up there to belt out a few tunes. I kept that in mind. I wanted to embrace the family environment, similar to when I was younger.

The bistro didn't have the feral-ness of the front bar that could scare away half of this town and the next, probably. Instead, the bistro was an average-sized room closed off from the rest of the pub that opened up to a beer garden. There were tables of different sizes filled with couples to small families and larger groups.

The kitchen that served the bistro was a small room at the back of this pub. It was adequate enough to make all the pub favourites. I followed the woman in front of me as she talked about the business she owned. It wasn't until she led me up the stairs to the second floor, away from curious ears, did the conversation heat up.

'Okay, Connor, what's your last name?' Jackie didn't beat around the bush.

Her question came as a surprise that I didn't answer straight away. Maybe she didn't think I would respond.

'I'll find out sooner or later when you fill out your paperwork,' she said before I had a chance to form words.

When I found my voice, I said, 'It's Black.'

'Connor Black.' She rolled my name around in her head a couple of times. 'Eva and Preston's eldest.'

'Yes.' She knew who I was. But just how well did Jackie know my parents before they moved to Melbourne? Had Jackie's family owned this pub long? I remember our family gathering here throughout the years, but I had no memories of my parents interacting with Jackie. *Should I be concerned?*

'What brings you back here?' It was a fair question to be asked.

'A fresh start.' There was no way I could have a fresh start and lie outright to a person who had just employed me. But no way was I telling anyone about the hazel-eyed brunette.

'Do I even want to know?' Jackie raised both eyebrows.

'It's probably best you don't,' I answered with the honesty Jackie deserved.

'Right.' She exhaled. 'This is the second floor, and it's yours if you'd like it.'

'Thanks, but I already have a place to stay.'

'Just so you know, some nights are bitches and will wreck you. This piece of salvation will come in handy. Keep it in mind is all I'll say.'

'Right.' I looked around the open space that I never knew was up here. Never before had I seen a space like this above a pub.

The whole second floor was open-plan living. Only the bathroom and laundry were hidden in separate rooms behind the staircase. I wandered around the open space and took it all in. At one end was the kitchen and meals, which was closest to the staircase. The L-shaped lounge rested up against two support beams and separated the kitchen and the king-sized bed.

Next to the bed was a built-in wardrobe, and it separated the bed and bathroom.

What more could a guy want than a fully furnished place to relax and chill out in? The space was neat and tidy, with lots of room to swing a cat. If by any chance I didn't have the energy to walk back to Lex's, or what was my parents' old place, I could crash here. There was no familiarity or warmth, so it was unlike my sister's place. I didn't feel the same here as I did at my childhood family home. But I would be foolish if I threw away the chance to stay here, seeing as I had no car. Maybe I needed this discomfort to push me outside my comfort zone. Turn me into the better person I wanted to be.

Jackie didn't show me around. She let me wander around on my own, and she didn't move far from the top of staircase. I could see the whole space as soon as I stepped up from the last step. But I wandered around anyway. Once I'd finished, I made my way back to where Jackie stood and followed her gaze as she peered out the window at the house across the road.

'That's my house.' Jackie pointed across the road through the window. 'That's where you'll find me if I'm not downstairs, in my office. It's just me and two of my sons. I don't know where my eldest is, and their father has passed away.'

I nodded. What did I say to that? It was clear she didn't want to talk about it, the same way I didn't want to talk about my fresh start.

As Jackie made her way down the stairs, she said as I followed her down, 'Come to the office when you're ready to leave. I'll have your paperwork and keys ready.'

I made my way out of the employee-only area and back to the bar to sit down for another beer. I didn't take the barstool I vacated earlier in the front bar. I pulled out a stool next to Jackie's youngest son and sat down. It was quieter here in the back bar that serviced the bistro. Jackie's bartender son didn't hesitate to put another James Squire down in front of me.

I took a sip. Jackie's youngest child was doing his homework. I could see the cogs turn. There was something he wanted to say. 'Out with it, kid.'

He turned to me. 'You're really here to help out?' he asked, hopeful my answer was yes.

'Yeah. I sure am.' It seemed to be the right answer. Happiness filled his face. 'What's your name?' I was curious to see who was Jarryd. And who was Jason.

'I'm Jason.' The kid next to me said then pointed towards his brother. 'That's Jarryd.' But I'd already figured it out by process of elimination.

'We have another brother, but he hasn't been around in a while.' Jason said. 'His name is Jaime, he's the eldest, two years older than Jarryd and I'm two years younger than Jarryd.'

I'm not sure why I was told that, maybe there was a void that needed to be filled here at the pub.

I brought my beer to my lips and drank what was left in slow sips, taking in the bar around me. When I finished my drink, I said goodbye to Jackie's two sons and went in search of the woman who had just hired me.

I found Jackie in her office. As I stood at the threshold, I said, 'I'm on my way out.'

'My boys give you a hard time?'

*Did she really think two teenagers could hassle me?*

'Nothing I couldn't handle.' I smirked.

Jackie handed over an envelope and the keys. 'My sons mean well. Try to get that back to me ASAP.' Jackie pointed to the envelope. 'I'll see you tomorrow. Around ten, you can help with the keg delivery.'

*Great. Just great.*

# Four

I was dog-tired after my first week as I'd worked the night shift every night this week. It was my week to close up, my last shift of the week, and I didn't have the energy to drag myself to Lex's and the bed at her house that called my name. Without a set of wheels, the walk seemed too far tonight.

I checked all the doors were locked, put the money in the safe and turned off all the lights. It had been a long night, and it was now the early hours of the next day. Sleep was all but moments away.

I crawled the stairs to the second floor that had been fitted out into a one-room apartment. It was mine for nights like this when sleep called and all my energy was gone. Jackie was right when she said there would be nights like this. I stumbled through the darkness and crashed onto the bed without a thought as to my clothes or the doona to cover me.

I didn't know how long I had slept for or what the time was. The sun shined through the many windows on the second floor. My tired body had thought nothing of the blinds last night as I'd crashed on the bed, something I now regretted. Aching all over, I stretched out, not sure if I was ready to get up, when my right hand felt something or rather someone next to me.

I knew I didn't bring anyone up here last night. It was just me at the end of the night, and I was too tired for that shit. My days of chasing tail were over, not that this town had any tail to chase. I now only wanted one person in my life. Her memory floated past me in that moment as my fingers tightened around a body part I could only assume was a forearm. The forearm moved, then tried to wriggle from my grip. I tightened my hold, and I didn't let go. I felt my fingers sizzle at our touch, and electricity flew through my body. Caught off guard I missed another limb being thrown my way.

A fist landed in my eye socket, which I knew would leave a bruise and possibly sting later. But for this second, I wasn't worried. The shock my body received and the hum of electricity that radiated through it made me let go, and I slid from the bed to the floor with a thump.

I wanted to stay here on the floor and until I had more energy, but I couldn't be a wimp or show any weakness. I jumped up and turned to face the bed, and my brown eyes stared straight into hazel ones. We gazed at each other. I couldn't believe the brunette was here, wrapped up in the bed I had just slept in. I didn't even have to try to get her here. She just showed up out of the blue.

'Oh my God!' The quiet words left her lips, and it was the sweetest sound I had ever heard. Was she just as surprised as I was to find there was someone else in the bed?

*Get a grip,* I told myself.

I had no words to say to her. I wondered what she was thinking as I continued to take in her facial features. I hadn't seen her since that night, five weeks ago. Relief washed through me that she was a local, not someone who was passing through this little country town.

'I should go,' she said as she sat up in the bed. She pulled the doona to her chin and wrapped her arms around her torso. *Was she naked under there?* I couldn't help but wonder.

'Stay.' The word slipped from my mouth, but I needed to get out of here.

I was too close to her, and there was no guarantee I could control myself around her. I made for the exit. I needed to move down the stairs and towards the back door of the pub. But she didn't let me. As my hand reached the handrail, she spoke again, and I heard more of her sweet voice.

'Wait!' It was louder than the other words she had spoken. Something in her voice made me think she was panicked. This was something I had never bothered to pick up on with anyone I'd spoken to before. But she made me want to pay attention to her, learn her body language and pick up on her cues.

I turned around and faced the brunette who was still wrapped up in the doona. I took in her beauty and wished like hell I could kiss her, taste her pretty pink lips. But I didn't remove my hand from the handrail.

'Your eye?' she asked, pointing to her own eye with her finger.

'It will most likely bruise,' I told her honestly. A smirk played on my lips, but I didn't want her to think I was a prick, so I blew air out of my closed lips.

'I'm sorry.' Her fingers touched her lips, and she withdrew into herself. 'I didn't mean to fall asleep.'

There was a shyness about her that made her adorable. I would never tell her that, though. 'Don't worry about it,' I called over my shoulder as I took the first step down the stairs.

I made it out the door and a few steps closer to Lex's, deep in thought about the need to have some sort of motor vehicle, when I heard footsteps behind me.

I didn't need to turn around to know that the brunette had followed me.

'You really need to put ice on your eye,' she told me, like I didn't know what to do.

'I've been clocked before. Think I know what to do,' I reassured this beautiful woman.

'Okay.' But that didn't stop her in her tracks.

She kept pace with me, and I wondered if she was about to follow me all the way back to my sister's house.

'Angel.' Out of the corner of my eye, I looked at her to see what reaction I would cause. None, not even the tiniest bit, bothered. 'I've got this. I'll be fine,' I growled as I continued on foot to Lex's.

There was a need in her voice that sought my attention. 'Hey.'

I didn't stop to turn around and look at her. I continued down the footpath that would lead me to the main road and eventually farther down Melbourne Road to my sister's house. Her footsteps still followed me. I didn't know what she wanted. But I knew I needed a quiet day as I lazed on the lounge, and that was where I was headed. There was a need my body craved, which only silence, or the feel of a woman under me, could sate after the long week I had just had.

'Do you always follow strange men?' I wanted to shock her out of the stupor she seemed to have fallen into. I stopped, and she stood next to me. 'How did you manage to sneak inside anyway?'

'Jarryd gave me a key. He told me no one lived upstairs.'

*What was Jarryd's reason behind giving out a key to The Grand?* Then the angel next to me spoke again.

'I just want to make sure you're okay. I did just clock you, and your eye has already got colour to it.' She looked up at me biting her bottom lip.

'Shit!' I huffed out more to myself than to the beautiful brunette that stood next to me.

I really needed to get some ice on my eye to stop the bruise that would form, as eyebrows would rise and questions would be asked. It wouldn't be good for business, but what could I do? I was lost in my thoughts and almost didn't hear the questions she asked me.

'Where's your car? Or do you walk everywhere?' Her hands landed on her hips. I sobered, turned to face her and thought she was sexy as fuck with the display of attitude she was giving me.

'I don't have a car, and how else does one get around if they don't walk?' I took a step backwards but didn't break our eye contact.

'Oh,' the word fell from her full lips, and I wished again that I could kiss her.

I continued to walk backwards. I needed space between us before I did something stupid, like reach out, grab her, take her back up the stairs of the pub and fuck her. 'You take another step towards me, and I will drag you back inside and fuck you like you've never been fucked before.' I pointed to where we had just come from, the second floor of The Grand Hotel.

I wanted to shock her and when her mouth gaped open, I knew I had succeeded. I could tell by the gasp that left her mouth. But I also saw her pupils flare, and there was a look in her eyes that showed the thoughts running through her mind, contemplating whether she should or not. Take that step, that is.

'Are you always this forward?' She took that step forward because I knew if she was close enough, she would hit me again.

I couldn't deny her question. 'Yes.' I reached for the sides of her face and crushed my lips onto hers.

Her hands moved of their own accord and landed on my chest right over my pecs. She pushed slightly, but I held her face a little tighter as I swiped my tongue along her bottom lip.

I silently begged for her to open her mouth. I wanted to devour her in this moment. It was the only moment I felt that I would get to do this. Kiss her. You never got those first kisses again, and she might disappear and not want to see me again. I had to make my best first impression. Her lips opened the smallest of amounts, and I didn't hesitate to dip my tongue into her mouth and explore what was on the inside.

The electricity I'd felt as I'd laid next to her in bed this morning had come back in spades as I kissed the sweetest of lush pink lips. The electricity had ignited something inside of me that I had never felt before, and I felt I could never get enough of with another woman. I didn't want to let her go, but I had to face a reality that she might not even want me.

There was a moan that left her mouth as I pulled away from her. My hands stayed where they were. They didn't let go of either side of her face. I wanted to see the look in her eyes. See what she held in them for me. Like lust or pure distaste.

When her eyes didn't automatically open after our kiss, my thumb brushed her cheek of its own accord. My lips touched hers again, and I saw her eyes open. She was breathless and exquisite. I didn't waste a moment. I put her over my shoulder and carried her back towards the back door of the pub.

Taking my keys out, I unlocked the door and carried her up the stairs. Had I stunned the brunette over my shoulder? There was no fight in her limbs. No words had left her lips. When I threw her gently on the unmade bed, the air in her lungs was forced out, along with a little squeal.

I wasn't sure what reaction I wanted. But I would take anything as along as she didn't scream blue bloody murder. I kneeled on the bed and then covered her body with mine. I loved the way she felt under me right now as she fitted almost perfectly. I was instantly hard, but I knew she wasn't ready for me. That much I could tell by the petrified look that flashed in her eyes. This look told me that she had never been carried over someone's shoulder or thrown on a bed before.

I rolled off of her, laid flat on my back and stared at the paint on the roof. She didn't need to feel the hardness that had grown between my legs, which told both of us how much I wanted her. I had seen the look in her eyes that told me she was momentarily afraid, before I rolled off her. What I didn't see coming was her body moving closer to mine.

Her head landed on my shoulder. She stretched out her neck to kiss my jaw, and I couldn't help but wrap my arm around her. I half smiled, knowing she was affected by me. My eyes drifted closed. No one had ever been able to lull me into sleep like that. Did she know she already had me hook, line and sinker? If she ever did, I was one doomed man.

# Five

I didn't know what I expected when I woke up for the second time today. I didn't know how much time had passed since I'd closed my eyes. But when I opened them, I felt a wetness, then the sting. That was when I remembered I'd been clocked in the eye, and the wetness was melted ice in a towel.

It was the same eye Zach had punched not that long ago. That side of my face would always be tender. My vision was blurry, maybe from my eye, maybe from the melted ice. I blinked them a couple of times, but my vision only cleared a little.

I didn't want to get up and look at my eye. But I had to. I had to know how bad it looked. By the way it felt, I already knew it wasn't good, and I didn't want anyone to see me like this. I didn't want to have to explain what had happened. I didn't even know the brunette's name or that she'd managed to sneak through the employee-only area to get upstairs. She definitely knew this town a little better than me. There was a story as to why she didn't feel comfortable enough at home that she fell asleep in a bed that wasn't hers – even if she didn't mean to – and I hoped one day she would tell me.

The wet towel fell into my lap as I sat up. All the blinds in this apartment were drawn, and I was surrounded by darkness even though the sun still shone.

I should have known she would be gone, and that I would be alone when I woke. I needed to turn my frown upside down though, get up and make my way back to Lex's and be thankful for a couple of days off. My eye would definitely need it. There was one thing for certain that needed to happen after last night and being dog-tired. Now that I had decided to take Jackie up on her offer, I needed to leave a few things here: a cap, a change of clothes and some toiletries.

My eye wasn't good. That much I could see as I stared at the mirror in the bathroom. My two hands landed on the basin as I leaned forward for a closer look. The bruise around it had now started to come out. This woman had hit me with plenty of force. The puffiness around my eye had swollen it shut. More ice was definitely needed, now and for the foreseeable future.

*Fantastic*, I thought to myself. Jackie would be, without a doubt, pissed if she saw the state of my face. I needed to make a quiet escape. High tail my arse back to my sister's for a lazy afternoon of ice on the lounge and maybe the TV in the background as a distraction to drown out the thoughts of one hazel-eyed beauty.

But I didn't get to make my quiet escape or high-tail it back to my sister's place. I didn't even get to finish examining my eye when I heard light footsteps make their way up the stairs.

I wanted to leave the bathroom, stomp my way out to whomever was there and give them a piece of my mind. But as soon as I saw who had come up the stairs, I stopped in my tracks at the threshold of the bathroom. I didn't make a sound as I leaned up against the door frame and waited to see how this would unfold.

'Damn,' was the quietest sound that came out of the sweetest mouth.

She thought I was gone. The realisation sent a sensation through my body that made my lips twitch at the corners. There was a warmness inside me, in my veins, that made me believe she might want me. She stood with her back to me, maybe a little surprised that I wasn't where she expected me to be. She didn't know I was behind her. I waited. She was yet to turn around and head back down the stairs. When she did that, her eyes would land on mine.

This was my chance to drink her in when she was unaware. She looked different from this morning. She had showered, changed her clothes and straightened her hair. It was now in a ponytail. She wasn't the crumbled mess of clothes with the bird's-nest hair from this morning.

Her body now filled out black pants that hugged her legs all the way down to her painted toes, kitten heels and a lacy black tank top that covered her torso and showed no cleavage. What was underneath was yet to be seen. My imagination ran wild as I mentally stripped her out of her clothes. The mental image of her naked made my dick twitch and my balls tighten a little. I couldn't help but move my hand to cover my balls and reposition my cock, which was starting to harden. My hand did nothing to calm the storm between my legs.

Busted. Why did she choose that moment to turn around? Maybe it had something to do with the groan that had left my parted lips. I watched her eyes catch mine, move to my hand that still covered my balls, then move back up my body to my eyes. Did she just check me out? Drink me in the same way I did her? A soft laugh left her lips as she held two takeaway coffee cups in her hands.

'I thought you'd left,' my hazel-eyed beauty said into the silence between us.

'I was about to make my escape.' I moved closer towards her, and with her hands full, I took the chance that she may spill two takeaway cups all over me when I pulled her close and kissed her.

I pressed my lips to hers in what I hoped would be the softest of touches. I didn't devour her mouth like I did earlier or push this kiss any further. Just my lips brushed up against hers. I tasted the coffee on her lips, strong with a hint of caramel, and I saved that away in my memory for later. I wanted to keep it for when I knew I would need it. The 'mmm' that left her let me know she approved of my kiss.

'I bought coffee,' she whispered against my mouth. 'To say sorry for your eye.' She moved out of my grasp and over to the stools at the kitchen bench.

I followed closely behind and wondered if I would even get to drink my coffee, or had she claimed it as her own? She sat down and slid a takeaway cup towards me.

'I wasn't sure if you even liked coffee. It's a flat white, no sugar.' She didn't turn to face me when she said those words.

I took a sip of the hot liquid and let it slide down my throat. It was the same coffee I'd tasted on her but without the caramel. I would have coffee any time she bought it for me as long as I got to kiss it off her lips when she drank hers, just to taste the caramel from her drink.

'Thank you for the coffee, it's perfect. But you didn't have to.' I wanted her to turn her head and look at me.

She didn't. Look at me, that is. She just drank her coffee in silence. Just when I thought this would be awkward between us, she blurted, 'Where were you about to escape to?' Her coffee cup covered her mouth, and I wondered why she wanted to know. Was she interested in me?

I didn't answer straight away, but when I saw her mouth open to speak again, I said, 'Somewhere quiet.'

'Oh,' she breathed. 'I should go.' She stood from the stool and moved away from me, leaving her coffee on the bench. But she only made it one step away from me.

I left my coffee next to hers and stepped off the stool to block her exit. I stood so close in front of her that our bodies almost touched. Air left her lips and rushed past my neck, and I so badly wanted to taste more of her. All of her and not just that sweet mouth of hers. She made me want to do crazy things to her.

I wrapped my arms around her waist, cupped her arse and lifted her into my body so there was no space between us. Her legs wrapped around me as I carried her to the lounge. I wanted to feel her under me again, so I gently laid her down and covered her. Her legs didn't move from around my waist, and I didn't roll off her this time when I knew she could feel my hardness pressed into her. It never completely went away from when I'd stood at the bathroom door.

I moved her ponytail from behind her head and let it fall over the arm of the lounge. 'You should go,' I groaned, as I sank all my weight into her. I secretly hoped she didn't want to leave me just yet.

As my thumbs traced circles on her cheeks, she did the last thing I expected. She reached her arms around my neck and brushed her lips over mine. 'Kiss me.'

Before she had a chance to move or say more, I crushed my lips into hers. The force of my kiss pushed her back towards the lounge. My fingers moved around her face to tilt her chin up to me as I devoured her.

I kissed her much like earlier when we'd stood on the footpath. I waited for her to part her lips before I dipped my tongue inside. When she did, all the air left my body, and I couldn't help but push this kiss a little further. I wanted to see how demanding she liked it. I was hungry for her and wanted as much as she was willing to give me.

Our lips moved in sync as our tongues danced for the longest of time. It was the best kiss I had given and received at the same time. I found her tongue to scrape my teeth against, her lip to nibble on, and when our breath was ragged and our heartbeats were fast, I pulled away from her mouth.

'Can you let me up?' Breathless words left her as I lifted myself up and leaned back on my knees. She had copied my action and kneeled in front of me. Her hands cupped my cheeks, and her lips moved towards my ear. In between breaths, she panted. 'I want to switch positions.' She wanted her body on top of mine.

My body reached for her grasp as she stepped away from the lounge. The 'tsk' that left her mouth stopped my reach for her. I twisted and let my butt hit the cushions on the lounge. Her hand warmed my skin and pushed my chest down until my head also hit the cushions.

# Black Eye

I closed my eyes at the feel of her hand on me. I didn't question why she had moved away from me. Maybe she wanted to escape or drink the last of her coffee. I knew the moment she returned to the lounge as there was a sudden coldness on my eye. This woman had gone to get more ice. Then I felt her body slide over mine. She wedged herself between me and the back of the lounge and rested her head against my shoulder. I wrapped my arm around her and tightened my hold. I didn't want her to leave me when I closed my eyes this time.

# Six

How I could have been so stupid? It was a mystery even to me. I didn't know how it happened, but she wasn't there. I guess my hold on her hadn't been tight enough. I thought she would be here when I woke up, that she would still be wrapped up next to me. I wanted her to be here, if not in my arms, then in this apartment.

It hurt that somehow, she'd slipped out of the embrace I'd held her in. Not once, but twice now. Something about her did something to me. She provoked something inside of me every time I saw her. An emotion I thought I would never feel with another human being. But the more time I spent with her, the stronger my need for her grew. I wasn't a patient man, but she made me want to wait for her. In the past, I had always taken what I wanted regardless of how I felt. But in her presence, I wanted more of her, and wanting more of her, I would have to let her set the pace.

I couldn't deny how I felt any longer. She flipped a switch inside me that made me want to call her mine. I wanted to possess her more than I had a right to possess any one person. She made me feel things I wasn't used to. Feelings I didn't know how to handle. From the warmth of her lying next to me, to the emptiness of her being gone. I was pissed. But only at myself. My blood boiled through everything I felt. I almost snapped inside and became the Hulk. I was afraid I would even turn green as I fought for emotional control.

She had gone and left me twice in one day. I didn't know why she did the things she did to me, but I liked the way she felt in my arms. It felt good not to be the arsehole I normally was. But I could only be angry at myself that I didn't know her name or have her number. I could have asked her name and given her my number if I had been thinking with my brain instead of my cock. And now I wanted to contact her, tell her to come back to me. I wanted her in my arms so I could kiss her again and again.

I dragged my palms over my face, and the stubble that had grown there over the last week felt good under my fingers. I pushed my hands back through my wavy brown hair that was now longer, too. The towel that covered my eye was wet with just-melted ice. It had recently been replaced.

The little things she did softened my edges but didn't help to improve my mood or the case of blue balls I had started to develop. I needed to find a way to get over myself and her. How long could I be expected to go on like this? Did she really want to play cat and mouse? Was she worth the chase? My head spun as I tried to figure it out. Somehow, I didn't think I was meant to have all the answers.

Black Eye

I pulled my arse off the lounge and looked around. After one night, the apartment had started to look lived in. But I didn't live here. I didn't live anywhere. My sister's house was just a place to crash. This apartment was another. Something I knew I would have to change, and I knew I had to do it soon. A vision of a grown up, settled-down Connor Black was never how I'd seen myself until a hazel-eyed angel caught my eye. And boy had she started to change all that.

By the time I reached Lex's, my head hurt, and I just wanted to crawl into bed with my miserable mood. Instead, I manned up, swallowed a couple of ibuprofens and headed for the upstairs bathroom for a long, hot shower. I stripped out of my clothes and left them on the floor. They had her smell on them, but I didn't want her to linger on my skin. I let the shower spray massage my tense muscles, while my body wash and the water cleaned my skin.

The pain pills started to kick in as I made dinner. Tonight's menu, courtesy of Lex, who kept her fridge and freezer well stocked, was steak, three vegetables and a couple of beers to wash it down. With a full stomach, I was ready for bed. I dragged myself back up the stairs with a towel full of ice. I curled into bed, still in my shitty mood, and placed the ice over my eye. I fell asleep as exhaustion finally took over.

With a little rest I hoped I would improve, or my mood at least, but it didn't. To say I sulked all day on my sister's lounge with ice on my eye every twenty minutes was exactly what I did. The background noise of the TV drowned out the silence, but nothing could get the brunette off my mind, especially now I had kissed her multiple times.

I even stared at the case my guitar sat in, but not even my guitar helped my mood. All I managed to do was break a couple of strings when I strummed too hard. Great. By the end of the day, my mood hadn't improved, and neither had my eye. For the first time since I'd started, I wasn't at all that excited about work.

I knew when I showed up for work for my next shift and stood in the doorway of the pub office, Jackie would not be the slightest bit impressed. But what was I supposed to do? I couldn't hide from her. I had to own what had happened and face the consequences, even if I had never done that before. But my problems were my problems, and I would never expose them to anyone. That one hazel-eyed angel had clocked me fair and square.

After two days off, I stood at the threshold to the office with my sunglasses and cap in my hand and knocked, Jackie took one look at me and sighed out her frustration. I could see the curse words as they took form inside her head. She wanted to completely and utterly lose her shit at me. But she didn't. Jackie didn't let any of her frustrations out loud in front of me.

'Jesus, Connor,' Jackie finally said in my direction. Stepping closer to me, she took a look at my eye. 'Please don't tell me that your eye happened at work or because of work.'

Jackie gave me a hard time with everything, and I was grateful for it. It would make me a better man in the long run. It was why in this moment I shook my head. I was unable to find my voice and fight, not with Jackie, but for myself. I was defeated and didn't want her to know I was all tied up and twisted over a hazel-eyed beauty who I'd shared a bed with, kissed more than once and held tight on the lounge but who'd disappeared the moment I fell into a deep sleep.

'Do I even want to know?' Jackie asked to give me the benefit of the doubt as she took her seat behind her desk again.

'No!' The word out of my mouth was so harsh that even I winced.

'I should send you home.' Jackie's arms were folded over her chest, and I wondered where she thought my home was. 'Without pay,' she threatened. Her words were a little louder, and I knew she'd said them to bring me back to the present and away from where I'd zoned out to.

'Jackie, please.' I didn't want her to send me home.

I baulked at her to give off the impression that I really needed this job and the money. I didn't need either, the money or the job. The truth was I wanted to be here. I needed a job like this. There was only so much a university degree could teach you. You learned the rest by hands-on experience. That was what I got when I came to work here at The Grand. Under Jackie's wing, I was learning the best hands-on way to run a business. This one just happened to be a small-town pub.

I had learnt a lot in the short amount of time I'd been here. Jackie was teaching me every aspect of pub management. I had only been here for a week but knew there was still plenty I didn't know. Jackie and I worked well together and I'd become her right-hand man. It was a job, I was sure, she wanted to show the ropes to her eldest son, Jaime. But he was an enigma and I had yet to meet him in person.

I liked my job. I enjoyed the work I did. There was something about this pub that felt right to be here. It was something the businesses I'd owned and the places I'd worked before didn't have. Maybe it was all the memories this place brought back to me that made work different. Memories of a time when my parents had brought Zach, Alex and me here for celebratory dinners and would dance with all of us by the jukebox. Work that definitely had nothing to do with the hazel-eyed beauty I couldn't get out of my head.

Jackie's punishment for my black eye was the cleaner's job. She needed me to fill in while the cleaner was away. It was the perfect punishment for my eye as the hours Jackie made me work were tough. She threw every cleaning job at me. And I had four hours to complete the list she gave me from the crack of dawn to just before anyone set foot into the pub. But it also kept me away from the customers.

The customers. They were great for business. Me and my black eye – not so much. So, Jackie made me clean. I cleaned the bistro, wiped the tables, the chairs, and vacuumed and mopped the floors. I cleaned everything and made sure the pub was tidy. My shift was up by the time the first delivery was received. I had to be gone by ten a.m.

Jackie didn't want anyone to see me or, more pointedly my eye, and the truth was I didn't want anyone to see me or my eye either. This was fine with me, but it meant I didn't know what happened at night. I didn't know if anyone was feral or misbehaving out front and for that, I wanted to kick myself.

It also meant that I wouldn't get to catch a glimpse of her either when she came into the pub. To add to my torture, I didn't stay here above the pub either. There was no point when I worked the early-morning shift. I wasn't about to hang around a noisy pub all day when I could enjoy the peace and quiet at my sister's house. Glimpse or no glimpse, I was still mad, as she'd left me and hadn't come back.

I wasn't sure what would happen the next time I saw her. Would I try to make her mine? Or would I leave her alone? What would happen the next time she saw me? Would she ignore me and look the other way? Or would she find a way to get me alone and whisper sweet nothings in my ear that told me she wanted me? Wanted a relationship?

# Seven

Tonight was the first night in two weeks that I had been allowed behind the bar to serve customers. That was how long it had taken for the swelling around my eye to go down and the colour of my bruising to fully fade. When Jackie initially saw it, she wasn't happy, but she didn't question me. My black eye wasn't because of work, so she didn't push the issue. She had three sons of her own, so she knew when to push and when to leave space. For the space, I was grateful.

I surprised a few people when I turned up for my shift. My first shift back, and I was on until close. I didn't know if Jackie was still in punishment mode or not, but I didn't care. I was back. Customers and staff alike thought my two-week hiatus meant I'd chucked in the towel, packed up my things and left. Little did they know I didn't scare off that easily, and personally, I wanted to be here. Almost everyone was happy to see me. Those that weren't were the ones who liked to cause trouble. It was bad luck for them, as my leaving wasn't an option. I wasn't about to give up or in without a fight.

I was pumped to be amongst the pub patrons. It was a little busy for a Sunday night, but I went with the flow. There was an atmosphere around here that told me the rowdiness had finally started to settle down. I wanted to believe that I was making a difference, even if the inkling in the pit of my stomach told me there was bound to be a time when it all blew up in my face.

I thought tonight would be like every other night, and for the most part, it was. I poured beers from the tap, popped tops from the bottles and made cocktails like I was an expert cocktail maker. I even brought food from the kitchen and set the meals on top of the bar in front of happy customers. I had just finished with a regular customer when I looked up to survey the front bar. My stomach reached for my throat. How I managed to swallow it back down, I didn't know.

The easiness of the night had changed. She walked in with a few of the less-than-stellar humans I had kicked out of here in the past month. There was a look on her face that I had seen before. It was the same as the first time I saw her. She was less than impressed that she was here.

Her expression turned unreadable as she stood next to a man, that today, I could see the resemblance as her brother. I didn't know her well enough to read her body language, so I didn't. But I would be a fool not to notice that she wasn't overly happy.

Whether it was because she had seen me or her brother had dragged her along with him, I may never know. She wasn't mine and didn't need me to rescue her. As much as I told myself that was true, I knew if I took her away from here, she wouldn't complain. Her brother, on the other hand, may have an issue. Was I ready for that fight? That, I also didn't know.

It had been two weeks since she'd slipped from my embrace, and while I wanted to march right up to her and demand to know why that had been the case, I couldn't. I had work to do, and she was a customer, the same as the others that followed in after her. I turned my back, just like the arsehole I was, without a care about what she thought. I left the bar area and her behind. Jarryd was on tonight with me. He could tend to their alcohol needs.

I made my way to Jackie's office, knocked on the frame and stood at the threshold between the hallway and her office. 'Heads up. We have company, and not the friendly kind.'

'I'll be out in a minute.' Jackie lifted her head away from the paperwork she had in front of her.

I nodded before I walked away.

I wanted to go back to the bar and do my job, but I didn't. I made my way to the kitchen instead. Surely, there was a meal that needed to be taken out. But there wasn't. I had no choice now but to go back to the bar and service customers. I stood just out of view at our cleaning station and watched the front bar, but really, it was an excuse to watch her. Like the prick that I was, I couldn't help it. Jackie came up and stood beside me then questioned me. 'What the fuck, Connor?'

I snapped out of where I had zoned out to, but I didn't get to answer her. An altercation had started to unfold in front of us. Jackie stepped forward to assess the situation while I had stopped wiping the glass I was cleaning. I stood frozen on the spot, like the love-struck fool I had become.

Jackie moved along the bar towards Jarryd and stood next to him as she placed her hands out and gripped the edge of the bar. We all watched as my hazel-eyed angel was manhandled by her brother.

'Let me go,' she growled at him.

'No,' he spat back at her. 'We are here to drink!'

'You are here to drink!' She had gotten right in his face before she let loose, and her voice was deathly calm. 'Now. Let. Me. Go.'

With one hand around her bicep, the other hand made contact with her face. A backhand across her cheek. She didn't flinch. She didn't even move. She did, however, press her lips together. A scream never left her mouth. You didn't need to be too close to notice the tears well in her eyes. But none trickled down her face.

Jackie was quick to raise her voice. It was mean as hell. 'Lucas Campbell. Get. The. Fuck. Out. You're not welcome in here anymore.'

Lucas was quick to drop both his arms to his sides, and just like my hazel-eyed beauty hadn't even been here, she was gone. Through the door to the back bar and out of my sight.

I wanted to go after her, but I couldn't. I might be needed to help Jackie show her brother out the door. But Jackie didn't need my help. Lucas didn't even care that he had made a scene. He just turned on his heel with his friends close behind, and they were out the doors of the front bar, not in the same direction as his sister had left. Of that, I was relieved. That bastard should never touch his sister like that! What the hell was his problem!

I wanted to go after him and lay him out. Tell him never to touch his sister again. But I didn't. I didn't have that right. Yet. I wanted to go and find her and comfort her. But I didn't do that either. I didn't know what we were or where we stood. So,

I finished out my shift instead, cursing myself for my indecision.

The rest of the night was quiet. Jarryd and I were the only people left as I closed and locked all the external doors of both the front and back bars. Jarryd left me to cash up and turn out all the lights. I was too exhausted to walk back to my sister's tonight.

I grabbed my bag from my locker, the one I'd brought with me tonight that held clothes and toiletries. Clothes I planned to leave here in case I needed them. I dragged myself up the stairs and headed straight to the bathroom to wash the smell of alcohol off me, then changed into track pants and a tight-fitting white tee-shirt.

I dumped my phone and keys on the kitchen bench. Then I dropped my tired arse down onto the lounge, leaned back and closed my eyes as my head hit the soft cushions. The scene that had unfolded in the bar tonight replayed behind my closed eyelids. That woman knew how to invade all of my thoughts, like re-runs of old black and white movies.

I was lost in thought and didn't hear footsteps approaching. I should have been more alert, ready to fight, throw punches if it ever came to that. Be the ruthless Connor Black I'd always been. But I wasn't alert, I didn't fight, I didn't even throw a single punch. I didn't even register that someone had touched me until I pulled my head from the back of the lounge and stared at the part of me that was connected to the other person.

Her fingers were entwined around mine. Sparks travelled up my arm. I wanted her to always touch me if it made me feel this good all over, even now when I was tired. Her arm pulled mine. She wanted me to stand up. So, I did. I stood in front of her, let go of her fingers and pulled her into me. I held her tight against my body, my forearm locking her body to mine. I kissed the top of her head and in that moment, I never wanted to let her to leave my presence.

But I let her go and dropped my arms to my side. She took one step away from me. I wanted to cup her face, but I knew that was a dick move. Her cheek was probably sore. I couldn't help but stare down at her, even in the darkness I could see she was stunning. I wanted to whisper the words of how beautiful she was, but I didn't get a chance to. She had reached for my hand. She wanted me to follow her.

We moved closer to the bed. While I knew nothing would happen, my cock didn't get that message. He loved the feel of her touch as much as rest of me did. We had stopped at the edge of bed. She had let go of my hand and was about to get into bed when I pulled my tee-shirt over my head.

Just when I thought she was about to object, I placed my index finger on her pouted lips and whispered, 'For you.'

She held my gaze. I dropped my finger from her lips and left her in wonder as to what my next move would be. I didn't have any plans except to sleep, but my cock needed to also get that message. I stepped away from her, pulled the doona back and got into bed. I laid on my side, away from her, so she could have her privacy. I didn't know if she would take my tee-shirt and wear it, but I hoped she did. I hoped she got in behind me and wrapped her arm around me.

When I felt movement on the bed, I let out the breath I'd held in. I was relieved. She'd decided to get into bed behind me. She leaned into me and planted a kiss along my jaw just under my ear.

She whispered, 'Thank you.' Then she laid down and just like I hoped she would, she wrapped her arm around me. In that moment, I easily drifted off to sleep.

63

# Eight

I should have known that she wouldn't be here this morning when I woke up. The whole time she spent next to me in bed, her arm was wrapped around my waist, her fingers on my bare chest, as her cheek rested on my shoulder. I didn't dare move while she was next to me. Even though I wanted to roll her over and wrap her up in my arms, pull her back to my chest and hold onto her. I didn't. I couldn't. Her touch made my cock hard. Harder than I had ever been before, but she didn't need that right now. Not after the night she'd had in the bar.

I was still hard when I woke up. I had dreamt of her fingers, that her hand hadn't stayed plastered to my chest but had moved instead over my skin, down my hardened abs, to the top of my track pants. Her hand wouldn't stop there either. It would move down under the waistband to cup my balls and cop a feel of my hardness. She would wrap her fingers around me, not too tight and not too loose, her hand on me would be just the right amount of pressure. Then she would move her wrist down, then back up. Stroke me, over and over. Build me up to the best orgasm ever.

With that fantasy now stuck in my head, I pushed the doona away. I lifted my arse to push my track pants down and kick them off. I grabbed my hardened cock and stroked myself. Applied just enough pressure and hoped it would be the same if she ever did touch me. I knew it was my hand, but I wanted it to be hers. I wanted her to make me feel this good.

I moved my hand slowly at first. I wanted her to be able to build me up. When I couldn't take it anymore, I would encourage her to go faster. Then faster again. Until I couldn't hold it in anymore and had no other choice but to spill my release all over myself, my abdomen and my chest. I would call her name as my body shook.

My hand moved fast. My breath was ragged. My body stilled. Cum shot out of me. Covered me as my orgasm shook the length of my body. The tingles started at my toes and made their way up my body and when they got to my head, my eyes flew open. Never had my orgasm felt that intense before. I had slept around and given myself plenty of hand jobs. Never had I ever fantasised like that before.

I pushed myself up onto my elbows when I heard an almost inaudible gasp fill the space around me. I got up to check out the noise, or maybe it was my imagination. There was no one here. I moved into the bathroom, took the washcloth on the bathroom sink, ran the water until it was hot, then I cleaned myself up. I grabbed my track pants and pulled them on. I didn't want anyone but my hazel-eyed brunette to see me naked. On the pillow next to mine was my tee-shirt. I grabbed that too and pulled it on over my head. It didn't smell like me anymore. It smelled like her. She must have worn it to bed. I smiled from ear to ear to myself.

I made my way to the kitchen for the caffeine I needed to start my day. That was when I realised one had been left for me. I reached for the takeaway cup and took a sip. It wasn't the same as the last coffee I'd drunk, as this was sweet like caramel. She'd bought coffee but mixed them up and left her coffee behind. So, she was here. I wondered why she left. Was she the one who'd made that sound? How much did she see? How much did she hear? I knew I'd moaned Angel more than once. I wanted to know. Did it turn her on? To watch me? To hear me call her that name?

I put the coffee down, and it landed on a piece of paper. A handwritten note. An 'I'm sorry' and a phone number underneath. She had left me again. But she'd apologised this time. Do I affect her, like she affects me? I wanted to hope so. I sat down on a stool at the kitchen bench and reached for my phone. I opened up my contacts and added her number. Angel. I was a lovesick fool, and I needed to play this right if I didn't want to scare her away forever.

*C: Thanks for the coffee. It's a little sweet. Think I'd rather kiss the sweetness off your lips than drink this.*

*A: Oh my god. My coffee's so bitter.*

*C: Come back. We can swap.*

*A: I can't.*

*C: Can't or won't?*

*A: I need to get to work. Twenty kids are waiting for me.*

*C: Come on. I'll wait by the back door for you.*

*A: I can't see you.*

*C: Why, Angel?*

*A: Why do you call me that?*

*C: I don't know your name.*
*A: I can't see you.*
*C: Why can't you see me?*
*A: I've already seen too much.*
*C: How much?*
*A: All of it.*
*C: Angel. I'm sorry.*
*A: Don't be. It was hot. Especially when you called me Angel.*

Oh my God. She'd seen everything this morning. Nobody had ever caught me in action before. I should be embarrassed, but I wasn't, not in the slightest. All I wanted was to see her again. I didn't know how to respond to her text message. So, I didn't reply.

What I wanted to say was… *Angel, you have no idea how good you make me feel.*

But it didn't matter. I didn't get to type in my message, and bubbles on my screen let me know there was another text on its way.

*A: I can't talk now. I'm late for work.*
*C: Have a good day, Angel.*

She didn't reply, and I couldn't help myself. I was a sucker for punishment. She did something to me and I wanted more from her. I wanted to give her more of me if only I knew how. What I did know was that I needed to get her away from her prick of a brother. I would never raise my hand to her, and she deserved better than what her brother handed out last night. I would never hurt her, and I needed her to know that.

Which reminded me that I didn't even ask her about her cheek. I didn't ask her if she was okay after last night. And that made me feel like a dick. So, I sent her a text.

# Black Eye

*C: Angel, how is your cheek? Are you okay?*

I knew she was at work and wouldn't answer me. At some stage throughout the day, she would have to check her phone and when she did, she would see that I had texted her. Maybe I would get a response. Maybe I wouldn't. All I could do was hope I would get one.

I drank her coffee, even though it was too sweet. I couldn't deny the sweetness felt good on my lips, like I had just kissed it off of her. Man, I had it bad for her and I didn't even know her. Not really. The most we'd said to each other was via text message. And that was this morning.

But I wanted her like I'd wanted no other. I wanted to taste her. All of her. We hadn't done anything other than kiss. One proper make-out session on the lounge behind me. I wanted to talk to her, get inside that head of hers and get to know her. I wanted to tell her things about myself that I had never wanted to tell another soul. Never had I wanted to do that with a woman before. *What was wrong with me?*

I snapped out of the daydream I'd slipped into and got off the stool. I needed to shower and change. I pulled dark blue jeans and a grey tee-shirt from my backpack and put them on. I pulled on black socks and slipped my feet into my black boots. My clothes from last night needed to be rid of the smell of alcohol. So, I washed them. While I waited for my clothes, I made the bed and folded my track pants and left them on the edge of the basin. The tee-shirt I folded and slipped under the pillow she had left it on. I hung my clothes up to dry when I heard the washing machine had finished. I would need them for my shift tonight.

I grabbed my empty backpack as I wanted to leave more clothes here at the apartment. I was on my way back to my sister's place when my phone buzzed in my pocket. I pulled my phone out and grinned ear to ear. I had gotten a response from Angel.

*A: I'm okay. My cheek is fine. You don't have to check up on me.*

*C: If that were true you wouldn't have left your number.*

*A: Okay. Thank you. I have to get back to work.*

*C: I'll be at work until close. I want to see you.*

I knew she wouldn't answer me. But would she come past the pub so I could see her? Only time would tell. It was about time we had a face-to-face conversation. Plus, if I played my cards right and we stood close enough, hopefully, I could kiss her again.

# Nine

Business was slow tonight. When business was slow, like to-night, that was when the real fun happened. Or so I was about to find out. I was glad I'd decided to bring my guitar back with me this afternoon. Though by the time I got back here, I was a little late. I had laid down on the lounge at Lex's house and fallen asleep.

It wasn't something I normally did, but my body needed it. The shifts I had worked lately had thrown my sleep pattern all over the place. Now that I didn't work regular hours like I had in Melbourne, I needed to listen to my body more often.

I had just enough time to change and start my shift. There was no time to pull my guitar out of its case and change the strings I had broken. I would have to do that later. But if it stayed quiet like this, I might be able to bring my guitar down-stairs and fix the strings while I worked.

An hour had passed and business still hadn't improved. So, I made my way upstairs to grab my old beat-up guitar. I sat down on a stool at the back bar and placed my first guitar on top. Pulling the strings from my pocket, I replaced the broken ones. Jarryd stared at me from the other side of the bar, his hand outstretched for my broken strings. I placed them in his hand when he said to me, 'Nice guitar.'

My worn-out guitar that sat on top of this old bar was the guitar I'd bought at the same time Lex had bought her guitar. We were guitar virgins back then. She had just moved to Melbourne for university and wanted to play the guitar to help with her stress levels while she studied. She'd dragged me along that day to show me what she wanted to buy and damn if she didn't convince me to buy one too. So, we learned, and we played together whenever we had the chance. It was the one thing we did together, and we loved to show each other up on what songs we knew.

'You play?' I asked, once I had finished reminiscing.

'Both Jason and I play,' he told me, like I should have already known this.

'I'd like to see what you've got some time,' I said of his guitar skills.

'You're on.' Before I knew it, he was gone, in the direction I assumed that would lead him to get his guitar.

When I turned on my stool, not only did I see Jarryd with his guitar, I saw Jason as well. Heaven, help me now. We rearranged the pub furniture so we could all sit next to each other. I grabbed my guitar from the bar, sat down and placed the instrument on my lap. The new strings needed to be tuned. The boys did the same. We made a racket that wasn't cool and didn't soothe. It was what attracted attention, but only to tell you to stop.

'What the hell…?' Jackie moved closer to where we were set up in the back bar.

By the time she made an appearance, her teenage sons and I had settled into an acoustic jam. We strummed, we plucked and moved our fingers all over the fretboard of our guitars. Jackie smiled and went back to wherever she had come from.

Jarryd and Jason showed me the songs they knew. They played a song each and one together. The boys had pretty good guitar skills. I played two songs for Jarryd and Jason to show off my guitar skills. I played and sang 'Perfect Storm' by Brad Paisley and 'Play it Again' by Luke Bryan. I heard claps at the end of the songs I'd played and not just from Jarryd and Jason. A few patrons having a quiet drink clapped, and Jackie had also come out.

Jarryd, Jason and I played through a few more songs that we all knew before we closed the pub down early. I was grateful for an uneventful night. *Maybe tonight I would be able to catch up on some much-needed sleep*, I thought to myself as I walked around the pub to check all the doors were locked. I cashed up the registers and put the money away before I turned out all the lights.

I didn't see Angel tonight. She didn't come past like I hoped she would. I wanted to see her. She must have had other plans, or her brother took up her time. I debated with myself whether to stay upstairs tonight or not. But my feet had already decided for me. They carried me upstairs, my guitar in tow. But not into the darkness. As I moved up the stairs, I could see a light on. That was unusual. Someone was here.

I moved quietly and placed my guitar on the kitchen table, then I walked into the kitchen to turn the light off.

'Hey,' a quiet voice said into the darkness I'd just created.

I turned around at the sound of the voice, but I wasn't startled.

My eyes adjusted to the darkness and could see a figure on the bed. She moved to stand in front of me. My hands reached for her. One to her cheek and one to her hip. Angel breathed in sharply through her nose. Both of my hands were quick to drop to my sides.

'Angel,' I whispered and before she answered me, I turned the stove light back on.

I needed to see her. Her clothes were black from top to toe, but her feet were bare. I didn't care about her clothes. It was her face I needed to see. See why she'd made that inhale. My fingers curled over her hip so she wouldn't run away. I drank in her beautiful face. Her quick breath had come when I'd touched her cheek. When I looked at the spot I'd brushed over with my thumb, I could see her bruise. Her brother had done a number on her, and her cheek was a nice shade of purple.

'I will kill him...,' I whispered between clenched teeth, and she tried to protest. I placed a finger to her lips to stop her. '...if you let me anywhere near him.' It came out as a growl.

A tear fell from her eye and ran down her cheek, and I wanted to wipe it away, but I didn't. My fingers pressed into her hip. I was more than a little angry that she was hurt. But I didn't want to scare her away, so I locked my anger down and pushed it away.

'Do you want ice?' I eased the grip I had on her hip.

She didn't speak, just nodded her head. I pulled ice from the freezer, found a zip-lock bag, dropped the ice in and wrapped it in a towel. I entwined our fingers, pulled her towards the lounge and sat down. As soon as she was comfortable next to me, I held the ice up to her cheek.

At the coldness on her skin, she let slip an, 'Ow.'

'I know,' I murmured, right before I placed my lips on her skin and kissed her. My lips were still near her forehead. 'I know it's cold.'

'Is this what you did?'

I nodded. 'Every twenty minutes.'

I held ice to her bruised cheek with one hand while the other hand brushed her hair from her face. As I combed my fingers through her hair, I felt Angel's fingers wrap around my wrist. I couldn't help it. My lips moved of their own accord, and they kissed her chin, her nose and her un-bruised cheek. Her pouted lips told me where she really wanted my kisses. But before I reached her mouth, I moved Angel until she laid on her back, then I pushed my hips into the softness between her thighs. I knew she could feel how hard I was when she let out a gasp of air. That was when I made my move to cover her lips with mine.

Our kiss was soft and slow. She let me set the pace. My lips moved over hers, my tongue dancing along her bottom lip, then moved inside to find her tongue. Her hands found my tee-shirt and gripped the edges, the brush of her fingers on my skin making me shiver. When I pulled away from her mouth, she was breathless and gorgeous, with her hair fanned out behind her.

'You think I'm your perfect storm?' Angel had heard us playing guitar downstairs earlier.

I nodded my answer.

'Play it again, play it again, play it again,' Angel sang to me.

I wasn't sure what that meant. 'The song?'

'Your kiss on my lips.'

So, I kissed her again and wondered if she also liked that song.

'Stay here.' I motioned to this apartment when I pulled away from her.

'No.' It was barely audible. The shake of her head, I understood.

'Move in, and you could have the place to yourself.'

'What about you?'

'It's just a place to crash. I don't live here.'

'I can't stay here.'

'I don't want you anywhere near your brother.'

'I can't.'

'Can't or won't?'

'I don't want to be alone.' Her confession did something to me.

I dropped the towel that was wrapped around the ice and left it on the floor to melt. I picked her up, and carried her to bed. Pulling the covers back, I placed her on the mattress and covered her. I kissed her temple as her eyes fluttered closed.

'My tee-shirt is under the pillow.' I moved away from the bed and turned off the stove light. Showered. Even though tonight was a slow night, I could still smell and taste alcohol. I needed to wash it off. I pulled on the track pants from the edge of the basin. When I moved closer to the bed, I could see Angel had made herself comfortable on her right side, her sore cheek exposed. I got into bed behind her and saw she had changed into my tee-shirt. I grinned as I laid down, my chest to Angel's back, and I held on to her for as long as I could.

# Ten

I knew she wouldn't be here again when I woke up in the morning. It was our thing. I worked nights, and she worked days. I knew she stayed until she knew I was asleep, then slipped out of my hold before the sun rose. But today was different. She kissed my cheek before she left, soft lips on my skin that told me it was her goodbye. Had I gotten under her skin? Had I worn her down? The peck of her lips felt like I had.

I sat up in bed and rested against the bedhead. The first thing I noticed was the coffee cup on the kitchen bench. I was quick to get out of bed to taste what was in that cup. What had she left behind for me this time?

My lips pulled up at the edges into a smile. There was caramel in my coffee, but not as much as yesterday. Just a hint. How she knew I needed less bitterness and more sweetness. I would never know. I drank slowly, savouring the taste on my tongue. I let the warmth soothe me. I was ashamed of how much this woman had got to me.

I grabbed my phone and opened my text messages. I found the contact I wanted and started to type.

*C: Is this a habit you want to get into?*

*A: It's a thank you.*

*C: For?*

*A: Your offer.*

*C: I'm serious about your brother. No one should ever touch you like that.*

*A: Let me think about it.*

*C: I will protect you, always.*

*A: I don't know you.*

*C: We can change that, but I can't change how you make me feel.*

*A: Please don't push me.*

*C: I will never mean to hurt you, I promise.*

*A: That word can be broken, and I don't need anyone to make me any.*

*C: Angel. I'm sorry.*

Just like that. Our conversation was over. She didn't reply. With my coffee gone, I threw the takeaway cup in the bin. It was time to start my day. Time to make changes. Between work and my spare time, I didn't stay in one place for too long. This apartment and Lex's were just places to crash for the night. Neither were mine. But that was something I planned on changing. Today seemed as good as any to make a start on those changes. With my phone in my hand, I searched for the notes app and made a list of things to do.

Before I could start on my, 'to-do list', though, I had an apartment to tidy and work clothes to wash. Picking clothes from a pile I had in the built-in wardrobe, I changed into them. When the washing machine beeped, I hung my clothes. Now I was ready to get out of here.

On my way back to my sister's, I knew I would have to tidy her place before she decided to make a surprise visit. But my sister and her house weren't what was on my mind as I passed a woman's apparel shop that was between the pub and Lex's place. It was Angel who was on my mind. She was the reason I stopped. She was the reason I was curious about what was inside the shop. I moved towards the door, pushed it open and entered.

I was greeted with a hello from the woman behind the counter as she gave me a concerned look that I didn't know how to read. So, I ignored it as I moved around the store to find what I came in here for. 'Do you need some help?' she asked from right beside me, and I had no idea she had snuck up on me.

'I'm after some clothes…' I started but was interrupted.

'We sell women's clothes. You're in the wrong shop. The men's is at the other end of Melbourne Street.'

'Well.' My eyes found her name tag. 'Lucky I'm after women's clothes then, Shea.' I didn't want to be a smartarse to Shea, but she'd pushed my buttons with her attitude and now I was afraid I might lose my cool.

'Do you know what size?' Shea's attitude was gone.

'Afraid not, maybe this was a bad idea.'

'Don't be ridiculous.' There was a small knowing smile on her face.

'What?' Now I just felt silly.

'You know, I helped your brother out of the exact same pickle that you are now in,' Shea told me matter-of-factly. A full smile emerged on her face, and she looked like she might laugh at the coincidence.

I stared at her in disbelief. There was no way my brother Zach had done this before.

'I sold your brother a watermelon maxi dress, along with some other clothes.'

'Uh-huh,' was all I could say. I knew that dress. I remembered the night Harley wore it.

'I'll let you in on a little secret.' I had no doubt Shea was about to inform me. 'Zach had no idea what size Harley was when he bought those clothes. He used me. Well, my body as a guide.' There was a moment's silence, before she continued. 'So, this lucky lady, tell me about her?'

'Shea, that's personal, don't you think?'

'It's Connor, right?' Shea asked. I just nodded my head. 'Tell me, is she tall, or average height? Is she toned or not? I'm here to sell clothes, not help you figure out the answers to love or to life.'

'Shea,' I started, then stopped. I needed to think about this for a minute. What did I want for Angel? 'I want comfy. She's just like you for tone and height. What would you wear?' I couldn't believe I was about to trust Shea to pick me clothes for Angel.

Shea moved around the store to look for clothes. She was a pro at this. On the counter she put soft three-quarter pants that would be snug on her legs and a tank that would hug Angel's curves. Shea did another lap around the store, found what she was after, and brought it back to the counter. She had found me full-length pants and a top that looked like they could be pyjamas. But who was I to question the expert?

I wandered the store myself, while Shea folded the clothes she had chosen. I found a flannelette shirt that would look cute on Angel. I also found a tee-shirt dress that I thought she might like. I put the items in my hand on the counter in front of Shea. She questioned my choice with a raised eyebrow and a smirk. But the look I gave Shea challenged her to tell me the flannelette shirt and the tee-shirt dress were not a good idea. She didn't say anything except for how much I owed her.

I handed over my new card from the account I'd set up with the local bank. This account was where my wages were paid. I wanted a fresh start. No way was I about to use the money I got from the sale of my businesses. I needed this fresh start. I didn't want anyone from my past to know where I was. I didn't doubt that the lawyer I didn't need any more had a way to track my money and, therefore, me. It was why I didn't want Lex to touch my money until I had my plans sorted out. Well, at least my plans for the lawyer anyway.

'Good luck, Connor,' Shea said as she pulled me back into the present.

'Thanks.' I folded the edges of the paper bag down and placed it into my backpack.

'You're welcome,' she said to me as I left her store.

Next stop was the supermarket. It was time to restock. I filled my basket with the food I wanted to eat. I grabbed more than I thought I needed. Two full grocery bags were what I had to carry back to my sister's. Lucky for me the supermarket was on the way and not in the opposite direction.

By the time I reached the front door, my arms were dead. When I put the groceries down, my muscles were relieved. I pulled the keys from my pocket and unlocked the door. Once the groceries were away, I collapsed on the lounge with my phone in hand. It was time to do some research. I needed two things: my own piece of paradise and a set of wheels with a particular rumble.

The piece of paradise was easy to find, but the wheels with a particular rumble, not so much. That one, I might have to compromise on. I emailed an expression of interest on the property I'd found in hope of a response and a chance to take a look.

# Eleven

After two days off, I was pumped to be back at work. Or so I thought. It was a little busy for a Wednesday night, but I went with the flow. I was grateful the rowdiness, for the most part, had finally started to settle down.

There were nights I still quietly told people to go home, but I hadn't yelled at anyone since that first day. Most nights were good. Business seemed to be good. Not that Jackie would ever tell me. It wasn't any of my business what the books looked like, but I could tell by the foot traffic and how much money I handled. That was enough for me to know the pub was okay.

I thought tonight would be like every other night, and for the most part it was, until *he* walked in with his friends, those few less-than-stellar humans I had asked to leave here in the past month. There was a look on his face, and I knew it meant trouble.

I made my way to Jackie's office, knocked on the frame and stood at the threshold between the hallway and her office. 'Heads up. Looks like shit's about to hit the fan out there. Lucas Campbell is here.'

'I'll be out in a minute.' Jackie's eyes never left her laptop.

'Okay,' I said, more to myself, before I walked away. It was the first time Jackie hadn't looked me in the eye when we conversed, with me standing at the threshold of her office.

I made my way past the kitchen to see if there were meals to be taken out when I heard a scream, followed by a loud thud. The scream came from the direction of the bar, and the thud from the direction of Jackie's office.

I weighed up who needed my attention first. I checked out the scream to make sure it wasn't urgent. I needed to grab my phone from under the bar anyway. Then, I would make my way back to Jackie.

When I stepped back behind the bar, the front bar was in full view. Shit was about to hit the fan, alright. The quietness was gone. It had been replaced by the type of rowdiness I'd seen that first afternoon almost two months ago. But today was worse. The bar was quickly becoming a mess.

I grabbed my phone and watched as people scurried out the doors of the front bar. Pushing my phone into my pocket, I climbed over the back bar that served our bistro and counter-meal customers till close and bolted the door that separated the two bars. I needed to contain what had started to unfold in the front bar.

Rushing towards the other doors that serviced the back bar, I reached for the keys that were always in my pocket. I locked and bolted the other two external pub doors. I knew this day would come the moment I started to throw their raucous arses out. Now I had a shit show on my hands.

I turned and slid down the door I had just bolted. Before my arse hit the floor, I pulled my phone out. Time to text the one person I knew who would be able to help me, but who I would need to explain this mess to. I sighed to myself and did the one thing I had told Lex I said I would do. I contacted Zach.

C: *Zach, I need your help. I'm at The Grand Hotel. I don't have time to explain. I need reinforcements if you can spare any. Meet me at the back door of the pub.*

It wasn't long before I received a reply.

Z: *I'm on my way.*

I pulled myself off the floor to check on Jackie. I rushed past people as they made their way towards the beer garden exit. I didn't blame them. It would be safer if they left. It was the only exit I hadn't had a chance to lock yet, apart from the front bar.

I found Jackie on the floor in her office. I touched the spot under her jaw to check her pulse. It was faint, thready, but there. I heard the thumps at the back door that let me know my brother was here. I left Jackie on the floor.

When I opened the door, I found my brother Zach, his friends that had kicked me out of his birthday party and a man I had never seen before. But he wore the same black uniform as Zach.

I greeted everyone who entered through the back door, but no one responded. I guess they thought I was still a jerk. I didn't blame them.

'Connor,' my brother spoke my name to get my attention.

I looked up and took in the same colour eyes as mine. I tried to read his expression, but he gave nothing away.

Typical.

I didn't wait for him to ask. 'A shit show has broken out in the front bar.' I pointed in the direction of the bar in question. 'I need to get Jackie to the hospital. She just collapsed.'

'You have a lot to explain, Connor.' Zach hands were on his hips, and the family trademark one eyebrow was raised.

'I know and when this is over, I can sit your arse down and explain it.' I hurried back towards the office to get Jackie. I didn't care that I sounded like a dick. I just wanted this night to be over.

Picking Jackie up off the floor, I noted that she weighed nothing in my arms. I turned to make my exit and almost crashed into Zach. 'Can you take me to the hospital?'

'Where's your ride?'

'I sold it. I don't have time to explain. Can we just go?'

Zach opened the back door of the pub and unlocked his truck. I put Jackie in the back seat beside me as Zach jumped in and took off away from the back door in a hurry.

This country town's hospital wasn't far away. It only took a few minutes for us to get there. I gently pulled Jackie out of the car and put my arm under her legs. I didn't wait for Zach. I knew he would catch up as I walked through the emergency doors and yelled, 'I need some help over here.'

Two nurses rushed towards me with a gurney in their hands. I laid Jackie down as the nurses got to work on her.

'What happened?'

'I don't know, I just heard a thud. I guess she collapsed.'

'How do you know Jackie Thomas?'

'I work for her.'

The nurse who first spoke to me said, 'We need to run some tests. You are welcome to wait for her in the lounge, but we'll need a family member present to explain anything we may find.'

'You know she only has her sons. I'm not sure they will understand.'

Both nurses nodded and pushed the gurney Jackie was on down the corridor to run their tests. I didn't need to turn around to know that Zach was behind me. I could feel his presence. He was a little pissed.

'This isn't like the last time I asked for help.' My voice was a little harsher than I intended it to be. There was a silence between us before I said, 'I don't need you to bail me out. I'm not in trouble this time.' Some of my less-than-legit businesses had landed me in hot water, and I had ended up in Melbourne West Police Station lock-up. Twice, Detective Sergeant Preston Black had bailed me out. The last time though, I couldn't reach my father, so Zach had needed to bail me out. I knew he wasn't happy then and he was less than impressed now.

Zach didn't speak. He let me fill in the silence. 'From the moment I knocked on your door to apologise, I knew it was time for some peace and quiet in my life. Lex said I could stay at her house and told me to reach out. But what was I supposed to say to you? Hi. I'm sticking around. Let's hang out and be friends. It takes time not to be an arsehole anymore. As God is my witness, I try. Every. Single. Day.'

I took a quick breath and didn't give Zach the chance to speak. I just carried on. 'I knew from the moment I walked into The Grand that the clientele was feral. The day I wanted a quiet beer I told the rowdy ones to take it outside. From that day on I was hired for my ability to keep the disruptiveness at bay. The rowdiness, the feral-ness had finally started to settle down. Our regulars had started to enjoy the calmer atmosphere. I guess tonight karma found a way to bite me on the butt. I can't walk away this time, no matter how hard it gets. This job needs me as much as I need it, Zach.'

I had a shit fight on my hands, that much I knew. What I didn't know was how to deal with any of it. Nothing like this had happened before in any of the businesses I'd owned. Or co-owned with Zach as my silent partner. It was all new for me. Not that the pub was a business I owned, but I couldn't just do nothing. I couldn't let Jackie down. She had given me a chance even when she didn't have to.

# Twelve

This time, when I took a deep breath, I didn't get to say another word as my brother pulled me into a bro hug. I welcomed the affection he offered as he slapped my back. I held on maybe a little too tightly, but I needed for Zach to understand and not hate me.

'I don't want to leave her here alone, but I need to find her sons,' I said as I stepped away from Zach.

He nodded. 'Let me take you back to the pub, and we can find out what happened.'

I followed Zach out of emergency and towards his truck.

'Why did you sell your ride?' My brother asked me once we were inside the cab of his truck. The sound of his truck was the same as Lex's. The rumble provided a safety net of sorts.

'It was tied up with my businesses,' I said as I stared out the window into the night.

'You're serious about your clean slate?' My brother had spoken with Lex.

'Bloody Alex,' I huffed out.

'She wanted me to know you were staying in town and that you would reach out when you were ready.'

'She got that right.' I was annoyed that my little sister knew it would be a while before I spoke with Zach.

'I told you not to be a stranger.' There was a serious tone to what my brother just said.

'And without a ride, how was I supposed to do that?' It was a smartarse remark, but I threw it back at him anyway.

'Your mobile phone.' Zach let out a chuckle.

'Okay smartarse,' I joked, as my brother pulled up to the back door of The Grand.

When we both jumped out of his suped-up black truck, I saw Jason approach Zach and me. 'What happened to my mum? Is she hurt?' His voice shook as he asked about his mother.

'I don't know, and we have to find Jarryd so we can go find out.' There was no time to bullshit this teenager. He was too smart for any lie I could think of to tell.

I used my keys to unlock the latch and pull on the handle to let us in. I closed the door firmly behind me and led Zach and Jason towards the noise I could hear in the back bar. We walked past the office and down the hallway that led past the kitchen and to the bistro. When we reached the threshold of the back bar, Jarryd turned to face us, relieved we had returned with Jason in tow.

'Do I even want to know how bad the damage is?' I asked of the people we left behind.

'No,' they all told me in unison.

*Jesus*, I thought to myself and wondered what clusterfuck waited for me on the other side.

Introductions were made and hellos were exchanged between Zach and his friends and Jackie's sons. I knew all Zach's friends except Andy.

'Thank you, I appreciate your help tonight to get Lucas and his friends to leave and everyone out safely.'

'Jarryd just told us how things have changed since you started to work here,' Nick said to me.

'It's not as feral, and business has picked up,' Adam added to the end of Nick's statement.

'Looks like you don't want to be a wanker anymore.' Those words came from Brock.

'Great job I did to change things here. You can see my effort by the look of the front bar,' I said with an exasperated breath.

'Connor don't be so hard on yourself. This is business. Shit happens,' Zach told me like he knew that sometimes shit went wrong.

I realised I didn't know the first thing about business. How to run one and what I did now that shit had hit the fan. And I had a Bachelor of Business. What good was I in this situation? Was I too proud to ask for the help I needed? I hoped not.

'I didn't know you had a soft spot for this place.'

Zach's words surprised me, as I realised that this pub did have a special place in my heart.

'Yeah, this place holds a few fond memories. I remember Mum and Dad telling us they met here. Every anniversary they brought us here for dinner and they would dance right here next to the jukebox.'

Silence fell all around us. 'I'm going to check the perimeter one last time,' Andy said to no one in particular as he got off his stool and walked towards the back door.

His words broke me out of my stupor. 'Guys, have you heard from your brother?' I turned to Jarryd, then to Jason. They both shook their heads at me.

'Give me his number,' I said more firmly than I intended.

There was one member of the Thomas family that was out of the loop on their mother's situation. He needed to know, and I was obligated to tell him. Jason handed me over his unlocked phone, and I entered the phone numbers of the Thomas family into my phone. Then I sent Jaime a message.

*C: Jaime. Your mother's in the hospital. Meet your brothers there ASAP.*

*J: Who is this?*

*C: Get your arse to hospital and you'll find out.*

'Come on, let's go to see your mother,' I said after my message conversation with Jaime.

'Want some company?' Zach asked me as he put his hand on my shoulder.

'No, it's all good,' I told Zach as I made my way around to the front bar through the employee-only area. 'Son of a bitch.' I snarled to myself. I was going to fucking kill Lucas Campbell for this as well as for hurting his sister.

'Need me to handle any of this?' Zach asked. He was right behind me as he stared at the same mess I did. 'You should call the police and get an official report for what happened tonight.'

I stared blankly at my brother. He knew more about this than I did, clearly. Making a police report hadn't even crossed my mind. Maybe I did need my brother's help.

'Jackie's going to need all the support she can get. I want to be able to handle this myself, but I would be an idiot to believe that.' Or to believe that I was too proud to accept the help my brother was offering.

'Why don't you let me handle the police report and you can take Jackie's sons to see her?'

I handed over Jackie's keys to Zach to give him access to the pub. 'I appreciate your help. I'll deal with the insurance company tomorrow. I want to leave the mess until everyone who needs to see it, sees it.' But there was another thing my brother could help me with. We all stared in silence at the mess that had been made. There were broken glasses, broken tables and stools, holes in the walls. There was even a hole in the hardwood floor. 'Has anyone taken photos yet?' I asked. The sight of the damage made my temper flare. I struggled to control it as my fist hit the hardwood of the bar.

'Andy has already.' Zach held up his phone before firing off a text, which I assumed was to Andy. 'I'll email them to you, Connor, and send a copy to the police.'

I nodded my appreciation.

'Reach out, Connor, when the insurance is sorted. I can help with this,' Brock said as he came and stood next to me.

'Thanks, man. I appreciate the offer.' I put my hand out for him to shake.

I turned on my heel, picked Jackie's car keys off her desk and showed everyone out the back door. 'Thanks again, everyone. Your help was invaluable.' Zach, Brock, Adam and Nick all climbed into Zach's truck. Jarryd, Jason and I waved goodbye as Zach pulled away from the pub and headed back towards Black's Bar and Grill.

I tossed Jarryd the keys to Jackie's car as we crossed the road. He could drive us to the hospital. At the sound of footsteps behind us, we stopped and turned around.

'Connor! I found this young lady wandering around outside.' Andy stepped closer to me with his arm firmly around the bicep of one hazel-eyed beauty.

'Thanks, Andy, I can take it from here.'

Andy let my angel go, and she didn't hesitate to come and stand in front of Jackie's strapping sons and hug them.

At the same time that I spoke to Andy, Jarryd and Jason said, 'Mac.'

Andy eyed me cautiously before he shook his head and turned his back as he walked towards his car. I guess there wasn't anyone else hanging around.

Mac. I rolled her name around in my head, but I didn't dare say it out loud. I was stunned as to why she was out here. I wanted to reach out and embrace her, but something wasn't quite right. Under the streetlights, I could see her a little more clearly. She was covered in bruises. Her clothes were torn, and her hair was a mess. She didn't look like this the last time I saw her. Someone had done this to her. But how could someone be so damn callous as to hurt her like this? Not someone. Her fucking brother. When I got my hands on Lucas Campbell, I was going to fucking kill him.

Mac took a step back from the young men and swayed unsteadily on her feet. I reached for and caught her as she collapsed. I held this battered woman close to me. She was safe now. My arm swept under her legs. I gently squeezed her as I whispered sweet nothings in her ear and placed her in the back seat and got in beside her. The guys jumped in the front. With everyone inside, Jarryd put the car in gear and took off for the hospital.

# Thirteen

The doctors and nurses were still running tests on Jackie. As much as I wanted to stay at the hospital with her sons, I knew everyone would be more comfortable if we didn't stay here. Especially Angel. She had fixed her hair into a messy bun and borrowed Jarryd's flannelette shirt to cover her torn clothes and the bruises on her arms.

Jaime showed up to check on his mother, every bit as skinny and lanky as Jarryd was and Jason would be. The man wore dark blue jeans and a long black tee-shirt. I could tell he was annoyed that there was now a hiccup in his life that he didn't want to have to deal with. Walking away wasn't going to help the situation, but that's what he did. I was left to stay with his brothers, but I didn't mind. I knew by their body language at the hospital that they would be more comfortable with me hanging around. They had gotten to know me over the last couple of months.

As much as I wanted to fall into bed as soon as the car turned off and I walked up to the front door of Lex's house, I knew three other people behind me needed to be taken care of first. I pulled my keys from my pocket and unlocked the front door. Like a moth drawn to a flame, three tired bodies bee-lined for the lounge.

'Guys, upstairs,' I said, flicking my head towards the stairs. Both of them mumbled a response but moved towards the stairs anyway. I showed them the rooms they could sleep in. Both kicked out of their shoes and let the doonas envelop them.

I found Angel, or Mac, curled up in a ball on the lounge. I was also tempted to leave her there and find a blanket to wrap around her. But I didn't. I wanted her in bed next to me so I could keep an eye on her. Would she have nightmares from what she was going through? Her bruises would be temporary, and she wasn't seriously hurt, but how mentally scarred was this woman? And I wasn't just thinking about tonight, as Lucas had slapped her and bruised her face in front of patrons at The Grand. But what the hell happened behind closed doors?

'Angel,' I whispered in her direction. Her eyes opened at the sound of my voice. She reached for me as I reached for her.

We silently climbed the stairs, my hand in hers. I pulled her towards my room and closed the door. As much as I wanted to crawl into bed and sleep off a long night, I knew I needed a shower. I searched for boxer shorts and tee-shirts, something for both of us to sleep in. Angel took the offer of clothes, and I wanted to stay and watch her change in front of me. But I didn't. I couldn't. I wasn't that strong. And she'd been through enough. I left her to get ready for bed while I showered.

The shower was hot, and the water eased some of the tension and my body wash cleansed me and made me smell better than before. Angel was asleep when I returned to my room. I pulled the clothes I brought from my bag and left them beside the bed for her in the morning. I slid into bed and stared up into the darkness. As soon as my head hit the pillow, I waited for sleep to come. But it didn't. My eyes wouldn't even close. Too many thoughts ran through my head of what had happened tonight at the bar, and what had happened to her. Man, I was going to lay Lucas Campbell out flat the next time I saw him.

'Connor?' My name came out a little sleepily as she rolled from one side to the other. My name when she said it sounded sweet in my ears. I always wanted to hear my name from her lips.

'Yes, Angel,' I whispered as I rolled onto my side. We were face-to-face. Our noses almost touched. My fingers itched to reach out and touch her, but they stayed by my sides. I remembered what I saw under the streetlights next to Jackie's car. Angel was bruised. My fists clenched at the thought of someone hurting her like that.

'Kiss me,' Angel whispered, and I leaned in to brush my lips over hers. Once. Twice. Three times. I couldn't see her pout, not really. I just sensed it.

My hand moved automatically. It reached out and cupped the side of her face. I pushed my fingers through her hair and pulled her face towards mine. When I felt her tongue against my bottom lip, I let her set the pace this time. The moment our tongues met, there was a spark that started at the tip of my tongue and travelled through every fibre of my body. I couldn't help but shiver. Angel felt it, too. Her hand curled into the hem of my tee-shirt, her body inching closer to mine. Our bodies were flush, our mouths moved together and our tongues danced. I loved it when I got to kiss to Angel like this.

*I could get used to this.*

I wanted to roll her onto her back, and sink my weight into her, but I didn't get the chance. Angel's hands uncurled from the hem of my tee-shirt. The palm of her hand brushed the edge of my boxers, and I shivered again. Her hands were warm on my skin as they travelled up my chest and pushed my shirt up my body. I reached back with one hand and pulled my tee-shirt off. Our kiss was broken.

Angel's hand pushed my shoulder, pushed until I was flat on my back. She leaned in and pressed her lips to mine but didn't start our kiss again. Her lips left mine and travelled along my jaw to my ear. Her tongue licked my lobe before she continued her journey down my neck and along the top of my shoulder. She had stopped three times now to suck, nibble and lick my skin. Each stop a little longer than the last, and I knew she had left her mark. Her lips on my skin felt incredible, and my skin zinged wherever she touched me. No one from my past had been able to do what Angel did right now. Make me never want to let go.

She moved her lips from my shoulder to my chest. Her soft lips scattered hot kisses on my skin until she reached one of my nipples. Angel closed her mouth over one, and her fingers found my other. She squeezed the tip as she sank her teeth in. She hadn't bitten me hard but that didn't stop the movement my body made. It bucked, my hips leaving the bed, but Angel didn't stop the pleasure she was giving either of my nipples. Her tongue stiffened as she flicked up and down. Then around in circles, in one direction, then the other, her fingers matching the movement of her tongue. Then her mouth and fingers swapped sides. No one had ever made foreplay feel this good. If I didn't think I was hard before she started to kiss me, there was now steel between my legs. I couldn't help but reach out and stroke myself up then down as I wondered what her mouth would feel like as she sucked my cock.

'Angel.' Her name was just louder than a whisper. I didn't want her to stop, just warn her. This would go somewhere fast if her lips didn't leave my skin. But they didn't. My hands cupped her face and pulled her up to mine. 'Tell me you're ready for where this will end?'

There was a slight tremor in her body, and that told me the truth. She wasn't ready. The tear that escaped her eye and travelled down to my thumb made me roll her on to her side and pull her until her body was flush with mine. Her body gave a little fight as she panted. My lips went straight to her ear.

'Angel!' Her body went completely still. 'I will never force myself on you, and I will never force you to do things to me,' were the words I whispered into her ear.

There was a silence all around us before I heard her choke out a sob. 'I want you to make it feel good. I want you to make me feel good.' There was more silence. 'I want it to feel good. It's supposed to feel good.'

I wanted to show her just how good it was supposed to be. But right now, like this, it wasn't how I was meant to show her. Instead, I rolled onto my back.

Angel relaxed, then she rested her hands and chin on my chest.

'Angel, baby, you need to talk to me.' Those words had left my mouth before I knew it and now, I had to roll with it. 'Your words are everything. They tell me to start, to stop, to hurry up or slow down. Okay?'

'Okay.' More tears fell from her eyes.

It told me no one had ever been gentle with her. That no one had ever treated her like the princess she was. If gentle was what she needed, it would be what she got when she was with me. The pads of my thumbs wiped the tears from her eyes, and my lips kissed the tip of her nose.

'Will you make it feel good?' Angel asked like she wasn't sure if she should.

'Now?' I felt the nod of Angel's head under my palm. 'You want it to feel good? You want me to make you come?'

Angel nodded her head again.

'What did I say about your words, Angel?' This wouldn't happen unless she said the words I wanted to hear.

'Yes.' The word was barely audible.

'Yes,' I prodded.

'Yes, I want it to feel good.' Angel's words were a little louder but not the ones I wanted to hear.

'What do you want to feel good?'

'You. I want you to make me feel good.' Angel breathed in, and on her out breath she said. 'I want you to make me come.'

They were the words I wanted to hear her say.

'Let's get this tee-shirt off then.' And just like I had, Angel leaned back, reached behind with one hand and pulled her tee-shirt over her head. I saw her bruised arms under the streetlight back at the pub, and now again as Angel pulled the material over her head. I could see she was covered in different sized bruises like she was used as punching bag. Finger marks and fist-sized bruising and their colouring showed different stages of healing. I saw red for every bruise that covered Angel's body.

'Your brother is a dead man.'

'I know, if I ever let you near him. But I don't want to think about my brother.' Angel paused momentarily. 'I want to think about how good this will feel.'

When Angel stopped talking, I took my aim and moved towards her lips first before I moved down to her breasts. My mouth landed on one and my fingers reached for the other. I sucked hard and flicked my tongue, all while I rolled her other nipple in between my fingers and thumb. I couldn't help myself then. I bit down a little harder than I should have.

A gasp left Angel's lips, but she didn't tell me to stop, so I soothed the sting and let my tongue play with her nipple. My fingers and mouth swapped, and I gave the other breast the same amount of attention, only I didn't bite this nipple, just brushed my whiskers over her tender skin.

My lips moved over the mounds of her breasts, up her chest to her collar bone where I sucked, nibbled and licked her skin just like she had done to me. I moved farther up Angel's body until I reached her shoulder, where I sucked, nibbled and licked her skin again. I didn't stop there for long. I kissed my way along her shoulder, up her neck to her jaw. I brushed my whisk-ers along her skin until my lips landed on hers. I kissed her passionately, and she kissed me back.

Her fingers circled my neck and pulled at the ends of my hair that were longer than they had ever been before. I liked it a little too much. I lowered Angel on to her back and let my fin-gers learn the curves of her body. My thumb brushed over her nipple just to see what reaction she gave me. Her body bucked up. Her upper body left the bed. My hand moved further down Angel's body until I reached her hip and feathered my touch on her skin.

'Are you sure about this?' This was the last time I would ask.

'I'm sure.' Her voice was more confident this time as she pushed her boxers down her legs and kicked them off.

I brushed the back of my hand over Angel's hip before I moved between her legs. I needed to know how wet she was. How wet had I just made her? I ran my finger along the outside of her sensitive skin. The caress bucked her hips into the air.

When her bum hit the bed, I opened her legs gently and rubbed my fingers over her pussy lips to find she was more than a little wet. When she was ready, she would enjoy sex. Hopefully she would enjoy sex with me. I stroked her pussy up and down, working my strokes from her entrance to her clit at different speeds. I wanted to see how much I could tease her.

'Connor.' My name escaped her breathlessly as her fingers still pulled my hair.

Inserting my finger into her, I worked her G-spot. I knew she was almost there, close to the edge and about to fall off.

'Oh my God!' Angel moaned as my finger pushed inside her. I pumped in and out of her a few times before I added a second finger. Another 'Oh my God,' fell from Angel's lips when I felt her tighten around the two fingers I had inside of her, my thumb began rubbing her clit.

I leaned down to cover her lips with mine. Mostly to silence the moans that were about to leave her mouth.

'Come for me.' I broke our kiss to whisper against her mouth before I kissed her again. Hard. Like my cock. I was harder than I'd ever been in my life.

Angel's body shook uncontrollably next to mine. I didn't stop my fingers as they pumped in and then out. I wanted her to remember this, the first orgasm I ever gave her. I wanted her to ride out how this felt. Just when I thought her body had given its last uncontrollable shake, I pressed my thumb a little harder into her clit and rubbed circles around her nub of sensitive nerves.

'Oh my God,' she said over and over as her body started to shake all over again. 'What have you done to me?' she asked, panting with her arousal.

'Just made you come, not once but twice.' It felt good when she came on my fingers.

'Will it always feel this good?' she asked as I removed my fingers from her body. My fingers found their way to my mouth. I couldn't help but want to taste her. She tasted so good. I couldn't wait to put my mouth on her and make her come on my tongue.

'I can't promise that. But I hope so,' I told Angel honestly. 'I will always make you come first.'

Angel pulled me down towards her, her lips moving against mine. We stayed with our lips locked for the longest of moments before I felt exhaustion take over both of us. I pulled back from her to tell her to go to sleep, but she already was. I found the tee-shirt she'd pulled off and slipped it back over her head. I put her arms through the sleeves, mindful of her bruises and pulled the material over her naked body.

I moved Angel's body and moulded it into mine. I wrapped my arms around her and kissed her cheek, hoping my ramrod hard cock would ease up before I developed a bigger case of blue balls than I already had. 'Goodnight, Angel.'

# Fourteen

'What the fuck, Connor?' The words travelled up the staircase, waking me up. My sister's voice was tight, maybe a little pained. Something I couldn't tell unless I looked at her face.

Curled up in front of me was Angel, her arm tangled around mine. Was she still here because I woke up first? Had giving her an orgasm worn Angel out enough to make her stay all night? Did she feel that comfortable with me, a complete stranger, that she stayed a little longer each time?

'Do not move from this bed,' I all but growled into her ear.

'Who is that? Is she your girlfriend? Oh my God, I need to go.' There was anguish in Angel's voice as she tried to guess who was downstairs. My arm tightened around her, and my fingers reached for hers as she tried to move off the bed.

'Angel, that whirlwind downstairs is my sister. This is her house and the four of us have just crashed her peace and quiet.'

'Oh!' was all that Angel could manage.

'Go back to sleep,' I whispered in her ear before I kissed her temple. I got out of bed, grabbed my tee-shirt from the floor and slipped into it.

I made my way downstairs, not ready for the conversation I knew my sister wanted to have.

'Alex.' My sister's name came out just loud enough to get her attention. 'Everyone's asleep, or I hope they still are. Can you keep it down?'

'What the hell happened?' Lex asked me with sunglass-covered eyes. She hadn't bothered to remove them, and I'd paid no attention too. She was referring to why there was a stranger's car in her driveway.

'I know we were going to catch up this weekend and play guitar. But I'm going to have to cancel. I'll explain all later.' I was too tired to explain everything now that had happened since I last saw Lex, or to have her grill me.

'Fine,' Lex said to me. Something wasn't quite right with my sister, but I left it alone. 'I'll be at Zach's,' she told me a little more quietly.

'Thanks, Lex,' I said as I reached out to my sister and wrapped her up in my arms, hoping that my offer of affection would help make things between us less awkward.

At the sound of the front door as it closed, I heard foot-steps on the stairs. I turned to see Angel make her way down. I stopped her on the last step. My hands cupped her arse and picked her up. Her legs and her arms wrapped around me, and I wouldn't want to be anywhere else. I kissed her as I carried her towards my sister's bedroom and the ensuite attached.

I put Angel down between the two ensuite basins, and she didn't move. I guess she was curious as to what I was about to do. I turned on the tap, poured in the liquid that would make bubbles, and ran a bath my sister insisted be installed when she bought this house. I turned to face Angel, my hands reaching for her top.

'Connor.' Angel slapped my hand away from the hem of her tee-shirt. Her eyes wouldn't meet mine.

'Angel, talk to me.' I stepped back to the edge of the bath-tub, even though I wanted to reach out and touch her, rub circles on her wrist to calm her. But I couldn't. Angel didn't want to be touched.

'The bruises all over me are bad.' Her eyes still wouldn't meet mine.

'The bruises don't change how beautiful you are,' I said qui-etly as I watched her, but inside I was seething that Lucas had dared raise another hand to her. Her face was scrunched up, and tears had fallen from her eyes.

'My brother saw you kiss me. Saw you take me inside the pub.' There was a moment's silence before Angel continued. 'He found out I stayed the night with you. He wasn't happy.'

'Show me?' The bruises on her body were purplish-green, like someone had grabbed her, squeezed her hard and pushed her around. How many more bruises could there be? Hadn't I had seen them all last night?

'Connor,' Angel warned me, but I needed to know. I reached down and turned off the tap. The bath was hot and full of bubbles.

'Show me, Angel, or I find your brother and kick his fuck-ing arse for all the discolouration I can see on your body.' There was a hint of anger in my words that made Angel look up at me.

Angel slid off the basin, reached behind her, pulled the tee-shirt from her head and dropped it on the floor. With her hands by her sides, she pushed her boxers down her legs and stepped out of them when they reached the floor. I didn't stare at the curves of her nakedness. I stared into Angel's eyes. She stepped closer, but I was still out of reach. Angel turned slowly in a circle and that was when I saw the beginnings of a new bruise on her back, red edges and a deepening purple centre.

'Jesus, Angel,' I said on a sharp breath in. 'What did he do? Kick you?'

Tears fell steadily down her face as she nodded her response. 'He doesn't want me to get to close to anyone. He wants me as a plaything for all of his friends.'

'Angel, your brother doesn't get to choose who you sleep with.' *Who the fuck did her brother think he was?*

'I know, but Lucas grilled me about my sex life not long after he moved in twelve months ago, and ever since he's tried to set me up with all of his friends.' Angel sobbed into her hands that had come up to cover her face. 'When I kept refusing to go on the dates my brother organised, he ramped up his abuse towards me. I thought maybe I could get Lucas off my back if I went on one of his planned dates. The one date I agreed to go on was the one friend I had a crush on. I had seen Daniel around town before he started hanging out with Lucas. He was sweet, but sex with him was just like every other time I'd had sex. It was vanilla, and I didn't fall into bliss like I did last night.'

I pulled Angel's hands away from her face and pulled her down onto my lap. 'That's why you wanted to know if I would make it feel good?'

Angel whispered into my shoulder. 'Yes'

'I will never rush you. When you are ready, we can go as fast or as slow as you want.' I brushed Angel's hair from her face, but inside, I still wanted to kick the shit out of her brother. Then I picked her up, turned around and placed her gently in the bathtub. Angel splashed as she tried to protest. 'Stay, relax please. I want to go and check on Jarryd and Jason.'

I left Angel to soak in the bath then ran up the stairs and grabbed the paper bag with the clothes I'd bought her. Angel's eyes were closed when I snuck back into the ensuite. I left the clothes on the basin. She could choose what to wear from the clothes Shea had picked out. Or Angel could wear the clothes I'd picked on my own to add to Shea's choices. After what she'd told me, I never wanted her to leave my sight. I never wanted her near her brother again. Or his friends.

I showered and changed while I waited for Jarryd and Jason to wake up. I knocked on their doors and waited for them to stumble out. Both of them were only in their boxers when they made their way out. Somehow, they'd managed to undress. I directed them to the bathroom with a fresh towel in their hands. They could meet me downstairs when they were done.

When they showed their faces downstairs, both of them had propped themselves up on the stools at the kitchen bench. I pushed bacon and eggs in front of them to eat while I went and checked on Angel.

When I opened the door to my sister's bedroom, I found Angel on the edge of Lex's bed. She was wrapped up in a towel. I wanted to sit down next to her and kiss her, but I didn't. I stood with my back against the closed bedroom door.

'Connor, I don't have any clothes to wear,' Angel said as our eyes met.

'Did you check the bag on the basin?' I asked and waited for her reaction.

'You bought me clothes?'

'Yes'

'Why?'

'You really want to wear mine?'

'I wouldn't say no.' Her sass made me wonder what she would look like in my clothes.

'Angel, if it were my choice, I wouldn't let you out of my sight again.' I let my words sink in before I said, 'At least with these clothes you don't have to leave so quickly.'

Angel stood, holding her towel a little tighter. She moved closer to me and kissed my cheek before she retreated to the ensuite. I stayed plastered to the bedroom door, even when I heard her say, 'Oh my God.' It took everything I had inside not to move. When the ensuite door opened, she stood in the doorway in nothing but her underwear. New comfy black underwear. Bloody Shea. She'd snuck those in. Served me right, I should have checked the receipt.

Angel's words were a whisper between us. 'You bought underwear too.'

'Please go and get dressed,' I growled back. Angel let out a little laugh, and I couldn't help but adjust myself. This woman really got to me. In only her underwear, she was so damn sexy.

Angel didn't close the door this time, she just pulled out the three-quarter pants and the tank Shea had paired together. Both fit Angel perfectly. I owed Shea a thank you, and because I wanted to treat Angel like I princess, I would spoil her with more clothes from Shea's shop.

She pulled out the flannelette shirt and slipped it on. It looked good on her. Angel reached into the bag again and came away with the other two set of clothes. 'You bought me a dress and pyjamas?'

'I know you have your own clothes, of course, but are any of them as comfy looking as these?'

Angel shook her head.

'Now when you slip into these clothes, I hope you will think of me.' I held Angel's stare and smirked. 'They are not pyjamas. They're clothes for when you want to relax on the lounge all day.'

'Yeah, that's what pyjamas are for,' Angel told me.

'I wanted comfy clothes for you.' I just wanted her cuddled up next to me. Then those words slipped out. 'Maybe I just want you to cuddle up to me on the lounge.'

'That sounds nice.' Angel smiled at me. 'Thank you for all these.'

'You ready for breakfast?' I asked with my fingers resting on the door handle.

Angel nodded, kissed my cheek again, then whispered. 'Thank you,' and let me pull her into the kitchen to make her bacon and eggs.

# Fifteen

When I pulled into the hospital, I couldn't help but notice the car behind me. When I parked, the P-plated car behind me parked next to me.

Before Jason exited the car, he tossed out in my direction. 'I texted Jaime to say we were on our way over here.'

'I'm glad he's here,' I told Jason as I eyed both of Jackie's sons in the review mirror. Was I surprised to see Jaime? I would have to say yes. I really thought he would be a no-show after yesterday proved to be an inconvenience. Jaime was ten years younger than me, but everyone deserved a chance to change, the same way I did.

Jaime exited his car the same time as everyone in Jackie's car did.

'I must admit, I didn't think that you'd show,' I said to Jaime when we made eye contact.

'I don't know how sick my mum is, and we may not see eye to eye, but I know she would whoop my arse if I didn't at least check in on her.'

'No matter how tough this gets with your mum, I'll be here to help you guys navigate this. Okay,' I said to Jackie's sons, not just to Jaime. I couldn't very well cut and run now that shit had hit the fan at The Grand. I would learn a considerable amount from sticking this out and proving that I was worthy of being Jackie's right-hand man.

'Let's go inside, shall we.'

We all made our way towards to front doors of the hospital. Angel reached for my hand as soon as I was close enough, and I must admit I liked the way it felt to have her close to me.

The automatic doors of the hospital opened, Angel and I were the first to step over the threshold followed by the guys. I made my way towards the reception desk but was stopped by one of the nurses from last night that headed my way.

'You're the man who brought Jackie Thomas in?' the nurse said on approach.

'Yeah, my name's Connor Black.' I introduced myself because I realised I hadn't last night when I'd carried Jackie in.

'I'm Libby,' the nurse said as she moved closer to where we all stood. Addressing all three sons, she said, 'Unfortunately, your mother's condition continued to worsen overnight. She had to be flown to Melbourne for surgery. We tried to call, but no one picked up.'

'Oh my God,' everyone said at once.

'How high was her blood pressure?' Jaime asked the nurse.

'High, and with her erratic heartrate, it's no surprise she collapsed,' Libby explained.

'Has she always had high blood pressure?' I turned to ask Jaime.

Jaime nodded. 'Ever since Dad passed away and she's had to take on the pub all by herself.'

'How long has that been?' I didn't know why I wanted to know, but something had told me that Jackie was at her wits end when I first met her.

'Two years,' Jaime said with the drop of his head.

'And how long has it been since you've been around to help out your mother?' The answer would give me the full picture.

'About twelve months,' the young man admitted. I could hear how hard it was for him to do just that.

'Thank you,' I said, so the nurse could continue to make her rounds.

'Before you go,' Libby said, 'let me get you the details of the hospital Jackie was taken to.'

'Thank you,' I said again and waited for her to write down the details and bring them back to me.

With the details in my hand, I made my exit. Once I reached the car, I unlocked it. But nobody got in.

'Guys, there are a few things at the pub that I need to take care of. Once that's done, we can all go to Melbourne to see your mother.'

'What about the pub? It's all my mum has,' Jason said as he pointed his anxious face my way.

'Right now, it's closed, until the insurance pays to have everything in the front bar fixed.'

'What about all our staff?' Jarryd asked me with a concerned look on his face.

'I'm going to take care of it all,' I said to reassure all the faces that looked my way.

When her sons heard the words, they offered small, appreciative smiles then got into the car. Angel squeezed my hand then let go to get into Jackie's car.

'What about me?' Jaime asked, but it was up to him what he wanted to do.

'You tell me,' I threw at the eldest Thomas child. 'You have a choice, stay here and oversee the work that needs to be done at the pub, or you could drive yourself to Melbourne to check on your mother and help your brothers cope with all of this. Or if this is all too hard for you, you could continue to be a ghost in your family's life.' I know the words I said were a lot to take in, but Jaime had to grow up sooner or later.

'I was so hot-headed when I stormed out and left my mother to deal with the pub all by herself. I would be a fool now not to see that my family needs me, and I want to be able to help as much as I can. As for my brothers, they've grown attached to you, and you're better at this than I ever will be. So, I think I might stick around and do my part at the pub.'

I could see the cogs as they turned over in Jaime's mind. He was torn up over what would be the right thing to do, so, I was going to help him out here.

'You have a car, Jaime, a reliable one too.' My words caused confusion to set in on Jaime's face. 'You can come and go as you please between here and Melbourne. It's a three-hour drive away.' Confusion faded from Jaime's face as he realised what my words meant.

'Okay.'

'I'm sorry if your brothers feel more comfortable around me, but if you stick around long enough, they will come around.'

'Well, if it's okay with you, I'll follow you down to Melbourne, stay for a couple of days then I'll come back to help out at the pub.'

'Sounds good. I'll let my brother Zach know to meet you with your mum's keys.' I stuck my hand out for Jaime to shake.

I took Jarryd and Jason back to The Grand. It was another quiet ride to our destination. I parked in the driveway of the house Jackie had told me about and got out.

'I don't know how long your mum is going to be in the hospital for so pack as if you will be there for a couple of weeks and don't forget your toiletries. Also, there will be a lot of downtime so include any electronics and books you want to read. And make sure you grab your headphones.' Jackie's sons nodded their heads as though they understood and took off towards the front door of their house. 'Jason,' I yelled as he reached the front door. 'You will need to pack any schoolwork you have. I'll be at the pub.'

I made my way towards the passenger seat where Angel sat and opened the door. I pulled her out, and we walked hand in hand to the back door of the pub. Once inside, I headed straight for the office. I found the details of the insurance company Jackie used and called the number.

The conversation was lengthy as I was not on the list to make a claim, but I explained that Jackie was out of action and that I was the next best person to deal with this dilemma. I owned multiple businesses and had dealt with making a few insurance claims before, whereas Jackie's sons may not have. They let me give them all the details of what happened, plus when they sent out an evaluator to assess the damage and take their photos, they would see for themselves how much of a mess the front bar of The Grand was in.

I made arrangements with the insurance company for Zach's friend Brock to do a quote for the repairs and send it in directly. I hung up and took a deep breath. I would have to get Zach to email the police report over for the insurance company. I would need Lex's help with this, so would text her later to give her the rundown. Now, I just needed to put together everything she would need to pay the bills, the staff and anything else that was outstanding. Lex would know what to do to keep the pub running better than I would, as this was more her area of expertise. Because in awful truth, I never kept a close eye on the finer details. I hired people to tell me my array of small businesses were running smoothly.

I grabbed a box that was delivered only yesterday with fresh fruit and vegetables inside and filled the box with Jackie's laptop and power cord. I gathered all the paperwork on Jackie's desk and put it inside the box.

'Jackie handled all of this,' I said to Angel as I pointed to the box and the paperwork inside. 'I made sure the bar ran smoothly.' I breathed deeply then let my thoughts out. 'I'm not sure how organised Jackie is, and what if my sister needs more than what I give her?'

'Leave your keys to the pub with your sister. If she needs anything, she can come and get it.' As soon as Angel finished her last word, I had her hands in mine and pulled them around my waist.

When her fingers interlocked together around my waist and I had my fingers in her hair, I brought her lips closer to mine and kissed her softly. But I had to stop myself before I went too far.

'You're right,' I whispered into her ear. The best thing I could do was let Lex handle the pub office while the Thomas' and I went to Melbourne to check on Jackie.

'I know,' Angel replied as she unlocked her hands and moved them up my back to hug me tightly.

Angel let me go and I moved towards the door, but she didn't follow me. When I turned back to face her, I saw the concern on her face. 'What about me in all of this?' she murmured.

'Your choice. You can come with me to Melbourne or stay here?'

'I really want to come with you, and I can organise it with work,' Angel told me, but I could see there was more on her mind than a trip to Melbourne and her work schedule.

'Spill it, Angel,' I whispered into her ear.

# Black Eye

'I can't go to Melbourne with only the clothes you bought me. I need warm clothes and toiletries.

'Angel, I will take you home to get your things.'

I reached for her hand with one of mine and the box with the other. This time she followed me out to Jackie's car.

# Sixteen

At Jackie's car, I loaded the box into the back. Before I closed the door, I saw both Jarryd and Jason stroll towards me with their duffle bags over their shoulders. The other canvas bag they carried I assumed held everything else. Everyone climbed in, and Angel told me her address. I followed her directions out past the irrigation channel the river fed into. After pulling up to the kerb outside her house, I got out to follow Angel. The guys made themselves comfortable in the back seat.

Angel didn't bother unlocking her front door, and I wondered why. She headed straight for her bedroom, a door she did unlock. Walking behind Angel I checked out her place. There wasn't much. This house wasn't decorated, and there wasn't any furniture apart from one leather lounge. Had Angel's brother sold her stuff or ruined it? What I could see was that Angel's brother was a slob who left dirty clothes and dishes lying around, and you could see Angel did her best, but it seemed like she was wasting her time. The guy really was a bastard, a bigger bastard than me. With the bruises Angel was covered in I wondered how long her brother had been abusing her and ruining the furniture in her house!

Angel pulled out her a dark blue canvas bag and the tote that matched. I sat down on her bed and watched as she moved around her room with a finesse I didn't have. She found and packed the warmest clothes she had. I made a mental note to buy Angel whatever she wanted, whatever she needed. She deserved the best, to be treated better than the way her brother treated her and more like a princess.

She filled her tote with her electronics, charge cords, and the novel and notebook from her bedside table. She moved into her ensuite where all her beauty products lined the basin, a moment later it was all packed into a toiletry bag. Next was her makeup, Angel picked it all up in one handful and deposited it into her makeup bag. Last were her hair products, brush, straightener and hairspray.

With her toiletry bag, makeup bag and hair products tucked into her duffle bag, Angel zipped it up. My hand reached for the handles before she had a chance to throw it over her shoulder. With only her tote left to grab, Angel took it in her hand, locked her bedroom door and led me out of her house.

On the way out to Jackie's car, I saw Angel's brother stalk towards us. Handing over her bag, I gritted out, 'Get in the car. I'm going to have a word with your brother.'

As soon as Angel was seated in the front passenger seat, I set my sights on Lucas. I wasn't in the mood to exchange any words so balled my hands into fists and swung upwards into Lucas's stomach. He keeled over, and I knew I had winded him.

Before Lucas had a chance to obtain any momentum, my left hand reached out to squeeze his throat.

'You're a dead man if you ever touch your sister again,' I growled into his ear before I let go of his throat, then pulled my right arm back to clock him square in the face. He was out cold on the front lawn of Angel's house.

Angel, Jarryd and Jason all watched on as I strode to the driver's side door jumped in.

'Wow,' Jarryd and Jason said.

'Oh my God, Connor.' She breathed out her displeasure. 'You knocked him out cold.'

'Your brother deserved it for the pub last night and all the bruises he's left on you.' I glanced at Angel before I took off to my sister's house, where I pulled in the driveway.

With the box from Jackie's office underneath my arm I carried it inside, leaving it where my sister would see it, in the middle of the island bench in her kitchen. Racing up the stairs while the others made themselves comfortable on the lounge, I packed everything I'd brought with me all those weeks ago. Then I texted both Zach and Lex to let them know what I was about to do.

*C: Hey, thanks again for your help last night. Jackie has been sent to Melbourne for surgery. Her three sons and I are about make our way down. I've asked the insurance company to reach out to Brock for the repairs.*

*Z: Take care, Connor. See you when you return. Hope Jackie is okay.*

*C: See you then.*

After this morning, I wasn't sure if Lex was still frosty. I guessed the only way to find out was to text her.

*C: Hey Lex, I'm sorry about this morning and that I gate-crashed your house with people you don't know. I have to go to Melbourne now. Hopefully I've left your house the way you like it. I have a favour to ask. The pub I've been working at has been trashed and the owner is in hospital with a medical issue. Don't worry about the mess of the front bar as I have Zach helping me with this. I need your help though, someone I trust to take over the office paperwork. I've left a box on your kitchen bench, but if what you need isn't in the box, I've left the pub keys for you to get in. I appreciate your help with all of this.*

There was no answer from Lex. I wasn't worried. She would get back to me when she was ready. Next, I was on the move down the stairs to round everyone up and get them into Jackie's car so we could drive to Melbourne.

'Jarryd text Jaime, tell him we're ready to go.'

Jarryd reached for his phone to text his brother. 'Jaime will be here soon. He also said he called St Vincent's hospital. Mum needs to have a triple bypass surgery and stents put in.'

My bags were the last bags to be added to the back of Jackie's car. I saw Jaime's electric blue Toyota Supra pull up to the kerb. Jarryd and Jason took up the front seats of Jackie's car, while Angel and I climbed into the backseats. A moment later Jarryd pointed the car south towards Melbourne and hit the accelerator, with Jaime Thomas behind us.

The inside of Jackie's car filled with conversation between Angel, Jason and I while Jarryd concentrated on the road and the left and right turns he had to make before we reached the freeway. Then he set the car's cruise control.

Jason plugged in his phone and found a digital radio station to listen to. The sound that played through the speakers was acoustic and both Jarryd and Jason sang along. Angel let out a soft laugh at the two teenagers enjoying themselves in the front, but she must have felt my eyes on her, and she turned to face me.

I didn't know what made the next words fall out of my mouth, but I couldn't help it. I wanted to know about the incredible woman next to me.

'How many times?' I wasn't sure Angel knew what I was referring to.

'What do you mean, how many times?' Maybe Angel was a little surprised I was about to ask her about her abuse.

'How many times has your brother abused you?' I clarified my original question. 'Everyone saw him slap you that night at the pub, and last night you showed up covered in bruises.'

'I moved here two years ago, and Lucas showed up twelve months later wanting a place to stay. He's family, so of course I wanted to help, but I thought he would move on after a couple of months.' Angel took a couple of breaths. 'But not long after he moved in did his constant badgering start, and when Lucas cottoned on that I was avoiding him, the badgering turned to abuse.'

Angel took a moment to collect her thoughts. 'My brother has always tried to get me to drink with him, and I have always refused. Lucas's pestering worsened after he questioned my sex life. He tried so many times to set me up with his friends. I was so angry with him. We would always end up at The Grand, and the guys would get drunk, and my brother wanted me to have one-night stands with his friends.' Angel paused, then told me. 'Lucas thought I would just go along with it. But I'm not like that, I don't sleep around.'

'The night you stopped, shook your head at me, blew steam out of that pretty little mouth of yours and stormed out?'

'Oh my God.' The words came out quietly. 'The moment you walked through the door and our eyes locked, I wanted so desperately for you to be my knight in shining armour, sweep me off my feet and get me the hell out of there. But you didn't. I was angry at you and my brother.'

I didn't answer, just listened to Angel. I remembered thinking she was breathtaking with her knickers in a twist, and from that moment, I knew I wanted more of anything she would give me.

'That night, I snuck into the employee-only area. I needed somewhere to hide until my brother cooled off. Jarryd found me, told me no one lived upstairs and that I could hang out anytime I wanted. He even found a spare key to the back door to give me.'

That explained how she had access to the apartment above the bar and why her split-second reaction was to slug me when I put my hand on her and tightened my grip.

'Lucas hadn't cooled off by the time I got back to my place. He was furious with me for staying out all night and not going home with any of his friends to have one-night stands like he'd wanted me to do. That was the first time Lucas more than manhandled me as he threw me around my house as a ragdoll. He liked to bruise me wherever he could get his hands on me, unusually in places you couldn't see, unless I was in my underwear, but when his abuse started getting worse he would dig his fingers in all over me, my arms torso and legs, twist my skin in a Chinese burn, punch me and kick me to bruise the rest of me.'

Something told me that while Angel wanted to keep the peace with her brother, she was starting to spend more time with me for her own protection. Maybe after last night she would never go back to living with him. I would still kill Lucas for what he had done to her. 'If I ever see your brother again, I will deck him for every time he's laid a hand on you,' I told this beautiful woman next to me as I reached out to give her fingers that rested in her lap a quick squeeze.

'Then my brother found out about us. I tried to stand up to Lucas, and that's when he bruised my cheek, his first public display of abuse. When I found his friend Scott on my veranda after I got home from work, I knew Lucas was up to something. I demanded Scott take me to him, but as soon as I got in his car, I knew I had made a mistake. Scott didn't take me to Lucas, instead he took me to a secluded spot and pulled me out of the car. He was rough as he tried to force himself on me.'

I clenched my jaw. I was going to kill that fucker too. 'Last night when my brother's security guard Andy found you?' But I already knew the answer. Angel was sitting here next to me covered in bruises.

'Yeah, I fought off Scott and ended up with a few bruises on my arms and legs, and my clothes torn. The rest of the bruises came from Lucas, as you know. When I showed up back at home in Scott's car he knew I'd fought off his friend. That's when Lucas attacked me and left me weeping and curled up in the foetal position.'

I did know. The fucker had kicked her, probably more than once.

I heard the sadness in Angel's voice as she quietly continued with the rest of her story. 'Lucas took off for the pub then. He wanted to take you down but knew he could hurt you just as much if he wrecked the pub.' Angel took a moment to even out her breathing before she said, 'These bruises, Lucas' abuse, the assault from Scott – I don't want to live like this. I should never have let it go this far, but couldn't see a way out before I crossed paths with you, Connor. Lucas has always been a domineering older brother, and I just fell back into old patterns, but now it's so much worse than when we were growing up. Especially when he drinks. So, on my way to find you last night, I stopped at Mulwala police station to file charges against my brother and his friend. By the time I got to the pub, all the doors were locked. I tried every door and was on my way to use my key on the back door when the security guy found me.'

I wanted to tell Angel that she never had to go back to her abusive brother and put up with any of the manhandling that she had copped so far. But I couldn't force her to stay with me. I had to show her everything would be better with me.

'I'm sorry I've upset you. But thank you for telling me.' I wanted Angel to believe I would never intentionally upset her, so, the next words that come out of my mouth were, 'You're safe with me, I will protect you. And if any guy ever lays a finger on you again, they'll have me to deal with.'

'I know,' she whispered in a voice that was now shaky, and I was glad she could see I would never treat her badly. Man, I wouldn't hesitate to knock out Lucas again. As for his friend Scott, if I didn't get my hands on him, I really hoped karma found a way to take him down.

Pulling out my phone I texted the one person who could help with Angel's situation – my father. He worked in law enforcement in Melbourne and would know how to help me help Angel.

*C: Could you please help with a dv situation? I may have left my woman's brother out cold on the front lawn.*

*D: Send me the details. I'll follow it up. Connor, don't want you making it a habit of this.*

*C: I can't make that promise.*

If there was one thing the angel next to me had taught me was that I couldn't make promises if I was only going to break them. I texted my father as much as I knew about the abuse Angel had received at the hands of her brother and the assault from her brother's friend. I waited for a reply to see if there was other information he needed. As busy as my father always seemed to be, I knew he would get back to me eventually.

We slipped into silence as we got closer to Melbourne. Were those tears I now heard from Angel as she curled herself up into a ball on the passenger seat? I wasn't sure, but I reached out to pull her closer to me and hold her in my arms. My touch must have been the right amount of comfort my angel needed, and I was grateful when all of her body weight sank into mine.

# Seventeen

The city had come into view, and we weren't too far away now. Jarryd navigated Jackie's car off the freeway and made his way to High Street through Melbourne city traffic until he reached St Vincent's Hospital, where Jackie had been transferred. Jaime was still behind us. For two country lads, they didn't get lost.

We made our way to the hospital on Victoria Parade for Jaime, Jarryd and Jason to see their mother. We first went up to reception as we needed to find out where Jackie was. Jaime made his approach to ask, as he was family, so they would tell him what we needed to know. The hospital was a maze of corridors and lifts that we had to navigate.

We finally found the nurses' station that the reception person told us to look for. Only it was unmanned. We waited a few minutes knowing a nurse was bound to return for us to ask where Jackie Thomas was. We didn't have to wait long. Her sons entered Jackie's room first. While she was happy to see

Jarryd and Jason, surprise dawned on her face when she looked at Jaime. Maybe she thought she had lost him but was grateful he'd shown up. I saw Jackie's face change again – she was surprised when she saw me as I leaned up against the entry to her room.

'Boys,' Jackie said as they all leaned over the bed to hug and kiss her. There was joy in her voice, especially at the sight of Jaime, but it wasn't hard to see that she was tired. I knew she was happy to see them, but she also had something on her mind. 'Can you please give Connor and I a minute.'

They released their hug on their mother and stepped back. Jaime and his brothers moved towards me at the edge of their mother's room.

'Stay.' I eyed the Thomas brothers. 'And listen to what your mother has to say.'

I stepped into the room and Angel followed me in. She stood next to me and held my hand, like she knew I needed her next to me as my lifeline.

'I told myself I didn't care about your past, Connor,' Jackie said to me as she laid in her hospital bed. I wasn't sure if she had had her bypass and stent surgery or was still waiting. 'But I found out about your reputation and the way you do business.' Jackie took a laboured breath. 'I have to let you go, Connor. My business is all I have. It's not for sale. You don't get to acquire it, take over, chew me up, then spit me out.'

I let the silence fall around us. I stood there and listened, let Jackie vent her frustration at what she had learnt about me. All of it was true. I couldn't deny her that. All of what I had done in the past was true. I did chew up and spit out all of my acquisitions. But not her business. I was never interested in taking away her livelihood. But she didn't know that I had sold everything I owned and now wasn't the time to tell her that either.

I liked my job and what I got to do at The Grand Hotel, probably a little more than I should have. That pub had changed my life and led me to Angel. I thought maybe one day Jackie and I could be partners. She had taught me more than a business degree ever had. Her business savvy and everything I'd learnt was something I would use as the foundations in my future business adventures.

There were so many things I wanted to say to her, to defend myself and make her believe that I wasn't that person anymore. I wanted to argue with her not to do this. But she had every right to kick me out. I could see from her point of view. It was the right thing to do.

So, I said nothing. I didn't argue with Jackie and when she finished, I mustered the courage to say with an even voice, 'Thank you for the opportunity to work for you. I will collect my things and hand in my keys when I return to Mulwala.' The hush that surrounded us felt heavy. Jackie said nothing, stunned that I didn't argue with her. But there was nothing left for me to say. So, I turned on my heel and left with Angel.

The young Thomas men were as stunned as I was that their mother had fired me. But they didn't know about the things I had done in my past. They only knew the me that had decided he needed a clean slate. I could tell Jarryd and Jason were angry that I wouldn't be around anymore, and I would miss those guys. Jaime was confused, as he didn't know what had been happening at the pub. It was hard to know what went on when you weren't around. But I also knew Jaime was pissed because I wouldn't be there to help him while his mother recovered.

I didn't know how to deal with their frustrations or help them, so I didn't. I had my own frustrations to deal with. I continued to walk past the Thomas men and find the exit.

Angel stood next to me the whole time and held my hand, her fingers entwined with mine. She was part of the reason I didn't interrupt and kept my mouth shut. I knew she could feel my frustration, but I wanted to be out of the hospital before I let any of it out.

'Fuck,' I heard myself say as I stepped out on to the footpath and into the sunshine of Melbourne's weather.

'Connor,' Angel said my name in a way that comforted me. She stood in front of me, her hands on my chest, her lips caressing mine. 'Jackie needed to blow off steam, and you were her scapegoat. She'll come around. Don't give up on her or that pub.'

'What if I have taken over? It's not to buy her out, but so she has a business to go back to. Jackie doesn't even know about the state of the front bar at The Grand, or that I've called the insurance company or that my brother Zach had called the police and had his head of security take photos of the mess. Or that I've asked my sister to help with the office. Jackie collapsed right when your brother stormed in.' My words rushed out, and my frustration was still evident. I didn't know what I would do now.

As soon as the words had left my mouth, I felt lips cover mine, and I let the heady feeling melt away my anger and blossom into what I hoped would be love with Angel.

When Angel pulled her lips away from mine, she said, 'Jackie will hear all about the things you're about to do and she will see when she sits down at her desk that everything has been taken care of and her livelihood isn't trashed anymore.'

'I hope you're right.'

Angel kissed my lips again to reassure me.

'You'll see,' were her famous last words.

We made our way on foot away from the hospital, hand in hand. I had a phone call to make and a favour to ask because, in my haste to get everyone to Melbourne, I hadn't organised a place to stay.

We made it to the corner of Brunswick Street and Victoria Parade before Jaime caught up and stopped us. 'Connor, wait.'

Both Angel and I turned around at the sound of my name. Jaime had followed us out. 'My mother might not need you, but I don't think I can do this by myself.' But was Jaime serious enough?

'Are you thinking about sticking around and helping out?' I asked Jaime. I wanted to know what his intentions were before I fully committed to helping out behind the scenes.

'My mother left me no choice, and from what Jason and Jarryd tell me, things have picked up since you've been around. There are fewer rowdy customers and more families. That's something I want to continue. A friendly family-orientated pub, as it's Mum's dream. Dad just wanted the business. He served anyone. Hence, what's been happening after five.'

'Okay. If you're going to hang around and make a go of it, then the damage to the pub will need to be repaired before it can reopen. That will take at least a couple of weeks, maybe a month. Someone from the insurance company will need to speak with your mother. The police will also need to make a report for any charges to be laid against Lucas Campbell. In the meantime, I guess you'd better brush up on your pub skills, but Jarryd can help you with that. When the time comes, you will then need to be able to oversee the back bar and keep an eye on the bistro. If you need help, you can always ask your brothers. Jason is old enough to help out in the kitchen.'

'What about you?' Maybe Jaime thought or maybe he hoped I would defy his mother to hold his hand.

'I'll be around. I have things I need to take care of while I'm in Melbourne,' I informed him. 'You have my number, and you can call anytime.'

'But you'll be back, right?' Why did Jaime want to know if I would be back?

'Yeah, I'll be back. Mulwala has a way of pulling at your heartstrings and making you want to call it home.' I didn't have to look at Angel to know there was a smile on her face. I could just tell by the way she had squeezed my hand that she was happy about that comment.

'I gotta go.' Jaime shook my hand. 'I have accommodation I have to figure out.'

'I might be able to help you out with that. But I'll have to let you know.'

'Sounds good.' He turned and waved as he headed back towards the hospital.

I didn't know why I offered to help. But I couldn't leave them in the lurch all by themselves. I pulled out my phone and called the one person I thought I would never have to ask for help: my mother.

'Eva Black,' I heard when she answered my call.

'It's Connor,' I told her, only slightly nervous about what I was about to do.

'Sweetheart.'

That word got me every time. It made what I needed to do a little easier.

'Did you ever imagine that I would call you and ask for your help?' I said, curious as to what my mother's answer would be.

'I know Melbourne hardened you, but don't be too proud to ask for help, Connor. It will humble you.'

My mother had an instinct, maybe it was a parent thing, where she always seemed to know just what to say. And because I didn't want to be an arsehole anymore, I opened my mouth and let the words flow, 'I sold everything I owned, and I've been crashing at Lex's holiday house. I'm in Melbourne with the Thomas family. Jackie's in hospital and I need a place to stay. Any chance you can help me out?'

'Oh my God, is Jackie going to be okay?'

'I think so, but she needs surgery.'

'I've got a place in mind.'

I wondered if she realised I needed a place to sleep more than one or two people.

'Will it sleep five?' I hoped I hadn't pushed my luck.

'I need to run a couple of errands. I'll be free in an hour.' My mum rattled off an address. I was vaguely familiar with that part of Melbourne. It wasn't actually too far from where we were.

Thanking her, I hung up.

# Eighteen

All three of Jackie's sons met us at the cars in the hospital car-park not long after I sent Jaime a text about somewhere to stay. He and I navigated more city traffic to the address my mother had given me on Wellington Street. We pulled into an underground carpark and parked in the spots next to where my mother was leaning up against her black Mercedes C-Class 200.

I took a deep breath. *Here we go,* I told myself. I was the first to get out. The others seemed a little hesitant of the stranger I was about to approach.

'Mum.' As I got closer, I leaned in to give her a hug.

'Connor.' We exchanged kisses on the cheek. My mother held the tops of my arms and gave me the once-over. It had been a couple of months since we had seen each other. My mother was a sought-after psychologist and up until I'd sold everything, I was busy making a presence at each of my busi-nesses. I hadn't made much of an effort before today to reach out. She though looked the same as always, every inch the businesswoman in her black pant suit with her sleek shoulder-length jet-black hair. She was a Black through and through, by name and by nature.

As for me, I knew she could sense a change and not just by the length of my hair or the whisker growth on my face. The man who stood in front of his mother now had a few softer edges. He had started to grow into his thirty years of age. 'You look good, Connor,' my mother murmured, releasing me. I gave her my most genuine smile as I nodded my head.

I turned to the car and motioned for everyone to get out. Angel was the first, followed by Jason and Jarryd. Jaime exited his car at the sight of his brothers as they stood next to me.

After introducing everyone, my mother was the first to speak. 'No doubt it's been a long day. Come on. Let's get you settled.'

The five of us moved towards the stairs. My mother's heels clicked with every step she took, and her shoulder-length hair swayed with each move. We all followed her up four flights of stairs to the apartments on the top floor.

'Your father always said I was crazy for not renting out this apartment, and now I can tell him this apartment came in handy today.' I wasn't sure what she was on about, but I didn't question what she was talking about either. I wasn't here to find out the intricate details of the things she planned.

Eva Black walked up to the door, unlocked it and stepped over the threshold. We followed her inside and stood in the lounge room with a surprised looks on our faces while she walked around to open the blinds and windows.

Sunlight and fresh air flooded this top-floor apartment. I turned in a slow circle to absorb what I saw. I had to pick my mouth up off the floor when my mother joined us.

'You're full of surprises, Mum.' Her eyes snapped to mine, and I could see the smile she tried to hide.

'Connor, you have no idea the tricks I keep up my sleeves.' Spoken like only a mother could.

'Thank you for helping me out.' Being grateful felt strange.

'The apartment has two bedrooms.' My mother was never one to dwell on emotional moments. I guess that was what made her one of the best psychologists the Victorian health system had. 'And the sectional lounge turns into a bed in a pinch.' She handed the apartment keys over to Jaime then stepped closer to the lounge to show us how the bed folded out.

The guys took note of how it was done, while I stood in wonder as to how a two-bedroom apartment was meant to sleep five. Eva Black in all of her coolness said, 'I can hear the cogs turning from here, Connor.'

'I'm just curious as to how this apartment is meant to sleep five?' I felt like I had just asked the dumbest question ever.

'It's not.' I couldn't say the words from her comforted me. I still felt stupid.

'Oh.'

'Connor, why don't we let the boys fight over who gets the lounge.' My mum gestured that Angel and I follow her.

Out of the apartment and down one flight of stairs, Eva Black stood in the middle of the walkway between the two apartments on this floor. She moved to the apartment that was directly under the one the guys would stay in, and unlocked and opened the door.

Angel followed her inside, while I stood on the threshold a little hesitantly. From the doorway, my eyes followed my mother's movements as she opened blinds and windows to let light and fresh air in.

Eva Black had left my line of sight probably to go and open up the blinds and windows in the bedrooms. My eyes found Angel's. She was looking around in wonder.

'Angel,' I whispered in her ear. She shivered from either the name I had just called her or the fact that I had snuck up on her, my arms wrapping around her. But Angel didn't get to talk to me.

'Connor.' The way my mother said my name made me drop my hands from Angel's waist and turn around to give her my full attention. Eva Black took my hand and led me to the lounge, where we sat side by side. 'You need to know that your father and I never wanted to keep the decisions we made from you.'

There was a small silence where she took a breath. I didn't interrupt her. I was curious as to what this was all about.

'Your father and I own this building and all eight apartments. The two on this floor and the two above us.'

I thought I knew what she was about to tell me, but I still kept my mouth shut. 'There's an apartment for each of us, your brother, your sister, your father and I and now you. The apartment was never meant to be a secret from you. There was never the chance to tell you. With everything you have done since university, I wasn't ever sure that you would need a place close to the rest of us. But then you rang, and it made perfect sense just to tell you.'

I shook my head to clear the fog that hung around. I tried to absorb what my mother had just told me, but what came to mind was, 'This apartment is mine? Seriously?'

'The apartment is yours, provided you pay the utilities and don't trash the place.'

'I sold everything for a clean slate. I'm not going to be that guy that Dad has to bail out of lock up when I do shady deals anymore. Thank you, you have no idea how much of a headache you have saved me from. Now I don't have to stress about a place to stay when I come to Melbourne.' I leaned in to hug my mother.

'You really love it in Mulwala, hey?' Eva Black questioned me and my intentions.

I wondered how she knew about my need for a change, or could she tell by the way I looked at Angel that she was the woman who would keep me out of trouble? Maybe my mother had spoken with Lex. Between catch ups with my sister and the occasion my father had bailed me out, she had to have been told what I'd been up to. Even though I hardly reached out. Maybe my mother sensed I needed to do something different with my life that included a need for some peace and quiet.

'Yeah. It's lost its shine now that I no longer have a job, though. But I still love the change of pace.'

'Don't give up, Connor.' Eva Black smiled like she knew something only a parent could. 'Things will work out.'

'Right,' was all I could think of to say.

I choked on my words when I looked up to see the happiness on my mother's face. I could see she was proud of me. When I looked at Angel, I could see her happiness too, relieved at the words she had heard. For the first time in a long time, I felt like I might be on the right track. All I had to do now was not fuck it up. Maybe my mum was right. Maybe things would work out.

'I'm sure you two want to get settled, so I best be on my way.' Eva stood to leave but there was one thing I needed to do. So, I stood up next to her, wrapped my arms around her, the same as when I was a kid. A proper hug with a little bit of squeeze thrown in.

'Thank you for everything,' I said, then unwrapped my arms from around her. She placed the apartment keys in my hand then moved towards the door.

'I didn't get a chance to stock the fridge. An hour isn't long enough to be able to do that. The five of you will have to fend for yourselves.' Even though my mum was out the door, she paused and turned slightly to say what she needed to say.

'I think we can manage,' I said, as both Angel and I waved goodbye and thanked her.

I sat back down on the lounge and leaned into the cushions. Closing my eyes, I breathed in to a count of five, held for a count of five, then let my breath out to a count of five. Some-thing my mother had taught her three children early on when we needed to catch our breath. And I definitely needed this moment to catch my breath.

Angel had rounded the lounge to sit down next to me. She took my hand in hers and squeezed. She wanted my attention, but I didn't open my eyes. 'What did your mother mean when she said she wasn't sure you would need a place close to the rest of us?'

What did I tell Angel? Did she need to know everything I had ever done? If I wanted to continue my clean slate, I would need to be honest with her. But I didn't get to answer Angel. She had spoken again.

'What did Jackie mean she found out about your reputation and the way you did business?'

Personal questions Angel got to ask, just like I had asked personal questions of her in the car on the drive down from Mulwala. Angel needed me to answer. I needed to get my thoughts together. She needed to know that who I was then and the person who sat next to her now were two different people.

'Talk to me, Connor.' Still lost in my own thoughts I barely heard her. 'I want to get to know you.'

I brought Angel's hand to my lips to kiss her fingers. She needed to know I was present and not the million miles away I just was.

'I worked really hard through university to save every dollar I earned. At the end of my degree, I started to acquire a lot of businesses. I chewed them up, kept the parts of the business I wanted and spat the rest out. I used a lot of people and tried to hide the things I did so my parents wouldn't know. But I guess my mother knew more about me than she let on.' I stopped for a breath. 'I did a lot of shady deals and got busted more times than I care to count. I was an arsehole to everyone I came into contact with. That's just how I knew to do business. University taught me all the theory I needed to know, yet the people I associated with here in Melbourne after uni taught me how to be ruthless, and that's all I've ever known.'

'What changed?' Angel rubbed circles on my palm.

'You, Jackie and my brother, Zach.' The words came out in a rush as I stared at our joined hands.

'Your brother?' Angel prodded.

'I wanted to sign his girlfriend, who has an amazing voice, to sing regularly at The Groove to bring me in more money. When that fell through, Zach gave me a black eye for putting my hand on Harley. After that, I really didn't want to be beaten up for all the arsehole things I had done.'

'And Jackie?'

'She's the boss. Everyone knew she was the boss. I've never had a boss like her before, as I was always the boss – just not a good one. Jackie knows how to get the best out of people. She works hard and keeps everyone on their toes. Jackie's a role model I never knew I needed. She changed my whole way of thinking when it came to working, owning and managing a business.'

'And me?' I could tell Angel was curious as to what my answer would be.

'You stirred up something inside me the night you blew past me at the pub. I knew then that I wanted to see you again. I couldn't believe it when I woke up next to you that morning a few weeks later. The best thing I ever did was kiss you and take you back upstairs.'

Angel didn't respond to the words that I had spoken, and I didn't know how I felt about that. I brought her fingertips to my lips and kissed them again. Then I stood up. All of a sudden, I had energy I needed to burn off. Something about being in Melbourne stirred up butterflies inside me. I made my way to the door. Why was I a sudden bag of mixed emotions? Was I anxious? Had I opened up too much? Had I let someone in too far? I had never done this before. Let anyone like Angel in. I had never opened up like that before or told anyone anything about me. It felt good to share. I just hoped I didn't scare Angel away with anything I had told her.

# Nineteen

With energy to burn, I made my way down to Jackie's car. I grabbed mine and Angel's things from the back and dropped them off at 'my' apartment. My inner-city apartment. It sounded weird, even in my head. An apartment I never knew about until today.

Before I got too caught up in my own head, I jogged back down to Jackie's car and grabbed all of the guys' luggage. Two duffle bags and two tote bags. I carried them up four flights of stairs, and I needed to see if Jackie's sons had settled in. I also needed to hand over the keys to Jackie's car. As I no longer worked for her, I could no longer call dibs on her car. But on the bright side, Jarryd now had a mode of transport while he was in Melbourne, and Jackie, when she was fit enough to travel, would be able to be driven home by her sons.

I unlocked the door to my apartment and wanted to call out to Angel when I heard the shower turn off. I didn't know what level our relationship was at, so I turned around not sure if she wanted me to catch a glimpse of her naked. I made my exit and sat down on the lounge, leaning over to undo the laces of my boots then kick them off.

I let my head fall to the back of the lounge. Just when my eyes closed and I started to drift off, I let the exhaustion of today overtake me and pull me into a dream state. I felt a weight cover me and push me further into the softness of the lounge and just like in my dream, I took hold of the body that had straddled me, and I rolled her over, letting my weight cover her.

That was when I felt the tension, a wriggle that told me they wanted out. My eyes flew open, and Angel was there under me. I didn't dream that. Or did I? I moved quicker than I ever knew how, and I made my way to the bedroom bypassing the mess on the bed and heading straight for the bathroom for a shower. I needed a moment to process what had just happened.

I didn't hear her come in. I was too busy in my own head at what I had done or wanted to do. My forearms rested against the tiles on the wall as I let the spray from the shower cascade down my back. That was when I felt her. Her hands wrapped around my waist, and she pushed her nakedness up against mine. I didn't move this time, just let the feel of her fill me up. I had never felt this way. Could it be that I was in love? Had I fallen in love with Angel?

'I'm sorry,' I breathed out. 'It's been a long day.'

'No, I'm sorry,' Angel said against my back. 'I should've known that today would've taken its toll on you. I shouldn't have asked those personal questions.'

'Angel.' I wanted her attention before I turned around. 'Personal questions are how we learn about each other.'

She may have been surprised by my response, but it was true, even if she wasn't convinced. I didn't try to prove I was right. I was done talking. Angel was right. Today had taken its toll.

My right hand moved then, left the wall it rested against to travel a long her arm until our fingers were entwined. We stayed like that until the water started to turn cold, then I shut the water off and turned around. Angel and I were now face to face, although she only came up to my shoulder.

For every step forward I took, she took one step backwards. When the towels were in reach, she grabbed one to throw at me, the other she wrapped around her torso. She covered up my first real view of her naked body and leaned up against the bathroom sink. I wasn't shy and not afraid to share my nakedness. I let her watch me as I dried myself. Her eyes found mine, then they travelled down my body, paused at how hard I was, and travelled back up my body to mine.

Before Angel stepped forward and let go of her towel, I knew when she reached me that she would get down on her knees. What I didn't realise was that she would trail kisses from my chest between my pecs, down my body and over abs that were no longer washboard to my belly button, where she stopped.

There was a moment where nothing happened. Then she was on her knees, and I wondered if she had ever done this before. I sensed her hesitation.

'You don't have to do this.' Just in case she wanted an out, I could just pick her up and take her to the king-sized bed.

'Shh,' she told me. 'I want to.'

The next words out of my mouth were, 'Holy shit.' I hadn't expected that.

Angel had reached forward with her fingers, wrapped them around my hardened length and stroked me from the tip to the base. She stroked me one more time before she swiped her thumb over the tip of my cock. I felt every hair on my body stand on end, and that had never happened before.

'Fuck,' I grunted out when my body shivered, and that was just from the touch of her hand around my cock.

On the next shiver that travelled over my body, I looked down to see the smile on Angel's face, before she slipped her tongue out and flattened it against the underside of my cock to lick her way up to the tip where pre-cum spilled out. Angel swirled her tongue over the tip, tasting my essence, and more sensations ran through my body like a bolt of electricity.

'Fuck,' I groaned again and again.

Angel's mouth on my skin sent tingles all over my body, like my veins were on fire. This woman had been the only one to have ever made me feel more than just the hardness between my legs. She had made me feel more emotion and more sensation and sent the most electric tingles through my body. I wanted to believe this was how sex was meant to feel, how love would feel.

My sexy brunette didn't stop the movement of her hand. One more lick from base to the tip of my cock and her lips were around my tip. Her hands on my thighs, Angel pulled me into her mouth to test how much she could take. I wasn't surprised when she gagged, and I don't mean to brag, but I wasn't small. Angel looked up at me. There was another smile on her face. She must have read the desire in mine. Her pleasure in doing this to me was almost too much, I told myself as I thought of ways I would return the pleasure. I just hoped Angel would let me play with her.

I breathed in deeply, tried to catch my breath, and when I almost fell out of Angel's mouth, it was the smallest reprieve. Like she meant for it to happen. She took her hand and wrapped her fingers around the base of my cock, stroking up and down while her tongue went to town on the tip.

I felt my balls tighten, and the sensation grew the more her hand and tongue worked me over. More pre-cum leaked out of me, and I wondered if she liked the taste of me on her lips, on her tongue. Before I let this go too far, I needed to decide if I would let her make me cum this way, or did I stop right now and turn the tables so I could have my wicked way with her?

My hands moved from my sides and into Angel's hair. I tightened the grip of my right hand and pulled her away from me. I could see the pout Angel gave me as soon as her face came into view. I pulled her up onto her feet, brought her ear to my lips and whispered, 'My turn.'

# Twenty

As soon as my hand let go of Angel's hair and cupped her face, I felt her tense. Her whole body stiffened, and she wouldn't look at me. Did I just say the wrong thing? I wasn't sure. There was a reason why she tensed, and I wanted to find out why.

I moved my fingers to tilt her chin upward. I needed her to look at me. Then I brought her lips to mine, and I kissed her softly. My lips moved over hers, and when she realised I hadn't forced myself on her, she reached out her hands, placed them on my hips and squeezed them.

My hands covered hers, and I slid them up my body and placed her hands around my neck. Her touch stoked the fire that I felt not just on my skin but as it travelled through me, deep inside. The way I felt when I was around Angel made me want to pull her in close and hold on tight, and not just for now but for the rest of my life. My hands travelled back down her body, and I felt her shiver under my touch.

Picking her up, her knees dug into my hips. Her sex was now pressed against my belly button, my cock brushing along her wet entrance, and I knew he wanted in. But I needed to take my time and worship her. Revel in this because it had never felt like this before. And I wanted her to enjoy me. I loved the feel of her naked skin on mine as I carried her from the ensuite to the bed in the master bedroom. The apartment didn't quite feel like mine, so I couldn't bring myself to call it home just yet.

Somewhere between the lounge and the shower, the bags had been moved and the bed was now clear of our debris. I resisted the urge to throw Angel on the bed. I would save the toss for another time when we knew each other a little better. Instead, I opted to place her down gently on top of the doona.

'I love you,' was on the tip of my tongue, a whisper that almost left my mouth. But once those words were out, I couldn't take them back and I didn't know if I was ready for that. I didn't have much at the moment. All I had was money. I had no job, no car and nowhere I called home. I wanted to have that much figured out before I said those words. Especially to this woman, who deserved the whole of my world, not just an apartment my mother and father gifted me with.

I gently pinned Angel under me and brushed her hair away from her face. I didn't want her to move until she talked to me. Whispering, I locked eyes with Angel. 'Talk to me.'

'Oh my God,' Angel gasped, and I waited to see if she would elaborate. She didn't.

'If you're not ready, it's okay,' I tried to reassure her.

'I don't know what you're doing to me, but I have never felt this way.'

'Wherever this ends up tonight, it doesn't end with goodbye in the morning,' I said honestly. 'I want so much more. For you. For me. For us.'

The words I said rolled around like a rollercoaster behind Angel's eyes. A tear fell down her cheek as her emotions had gotten the better of her. Maybe I was too much for this woman?

I reached for the bedside table and found a packet of condoms I knew I hadn't put there. I peeled one off the string between my teeth and put the rest back in the drawer. Angel took the condom from me and held it in her hand. I wiped her tear away and kissed along her jaw. I moved to pleasure her body with kisses only as my arms pinned her in and held me up.

'This doesn't go any further unless you say so,' I said when I reached the shell of Angel's ear.

Her hands cupped my face, and her lips whispered into my ear, 'I want you. Make me feel as good as last time.' Then she pushed my head down to where she wanted me.

I let Angel move my head right down to just below her pubic bone, where I kissed the small amount of hair she had there. Words ran through my head to promise her, but then I remembered what she said about promises and I let my thoughts go. I told myself it was best just to show her.

So, I took the words that she gave me as a green light to go ahead and pleasure her body. I took Angel's hands from my face, and I held them up over her head, so I had full access to watch her squirm under the kisses I was about to give her.

I started at her wrists that I held in one of my own hands, and I kissed down the inside of her left arm. When I got to her shoulder, I tilted her jaw out of my way to get better access to her neck. I continued to kiss my way down Angel's body, stopping momentarily at her voluptuous breasts. I held one breast in my free hand while my lips, tongue and teeth went to town on her other breast and nipple.

When Angel breathed out, 'Oh my God,' I knew it was time to change over to the other breast. I swapped my hold on her wrists to my other hand as fingertips on my now-free hand traced a line down her right arm to her breast. My whole hand covered her as I closed my fingers over the full mounds and gave a little squeeze.

I kissed farther down Angel's body from the undersides of her breasts down to her belly button. The further down her body I went, the less I was able to hold onto her wrists, and eventually, I had to let go. I knew that as soon as I let go of her wrists, she would move her hands into my hair and push me down to where she really wanted me to kiss her.

I couldn't tease her anymore. The more I teased her the harder I got and if I wasn't careful, I would lose what I felt between my legs way too early. Once I was again down past Angel's pubic bone, I didn't stop to kiss it this time. I moved lower to the mound of her pussy, flicked my tongue out and licked all the way down.

On my way back up I flattened my tongue, which earnt me a 'Holy shit, Connor,' from Angel. I worked my tongue all over Angel's pussy until I felt her fingers tighten in my hair, a little tell, which let me know she was close to the edge. Then I let not one but two fingers run through her wetness, before I pushed both of them inside her. Angel bucked her hips. I had surprised her.

'Breathe, Angel, let it go, let me hear you moan my name.' I moved my mouth away from teasing the lips of her pussy.

Angel writhed on my fingers, then I heard her murmur my name followed by a few holy fucks.

Angel took a few shallow breaths and when I heard her take one decent breath in, I returned to her pleasure. I moved my fingers out, then in, slowly at first, then faster as I felt her muscles relax. Her hands had moved from my hair to the doona that covered the bed.

Angel scrunched the doona tightly in her hands as she fell over the edge of her climax with my fingers inside her and the flick of my tongue against her clit. She groaned out loud as her body shuddered right before me. When I looked up, I saw the most wonderful sight, with her arched off the bed.

One more shudder from Angel landed her on the bed. When her body no longer shook, and her sex muscles had loosened their grip on my fingers, she looked down to see me as I removed my fingers and licked them clean. Damn, she tasted so good, her juices so sweet on my tongue. I moved up her body and I couldn't help but stare at how exquisite she looked now that she was on the other side of her orgasmic release.

# Twenty-one

I leaned down to kiss Angel's lips. I wanted to tell her how breathtaking she was, but I didn't get the chance. She had ripped open the foil packet that held the condom. I smiled a half smile to myself. I had to give her some credit. She wasn't all shy. Out of her shell, she could give me a run for my money.

'I want to know if the sex is as good as your mouth and fingers,' the words Angel told me came out like she had run a marathon and were just above a whisper. Her words were a challenge I happily accepted.

I took the condom from her. 'Are you sure?' I rolled the condom on over my hardness that now ached to be inside her.

Angel nodded, but like I had told her before, I needed her to say those words to me out loud.

'Angel.' I stilled myself above her.

When the words left her mouth, I was the one who let out a stunned laugh. 'Connor, I want you to fuck me.'

I took hold of myself and stroked once up, then down. There was a buzz that ran through me, and I couldn't believe I got to do this, to be the first person to show her what sex was supposed to be like. I ran the tip of my cock through the wetness I had just created, and Angel arched a little.

I pushed away the storm that brewed inside my head, and I looked at her. I told myself that if I did this, there was no turning back. This woman would be it for me. She made me feel like this could be love. So, what I was about to do one time with Angel would never be enough. I just hoped it was the same for her. I ran my tip through her wetness one more time, and like my cock had had sex with her before, it lined itself up to her entrance and pushed its tip inside.

'Ohhh,' was the gasp that left Angel's mouth.

Maybe she wasn't ready for me. Her arms circled my neck and pulled me down to her. 'Is that all you got? Or is there more?' I liked the little minx that came out now she was under me. At the cheek Angel gave me, I couldn't help but reach out and pinch her nipple, 'Ah,' she groaned, and I thought she might even like the sting she now felt.

I took my other hand and cupped her cheek, tilting her chin up to give me the best access to kiss her hard. I claimed her mouth this time as I pushed my cock all the way in and stopped. My lips swallowed the words, or the groan of what was just about to fall from her mouth. Maybe there was a little sass that was about to come out, but my kiss stopped that.

My lips hovered over hers as I made my first move out and then back in. I wanted to see the look on her face as I filled her up. There was a flare of desire as I stared into slightly darker hazel eyes, and could Angel see the desire in mine? This beautiful woman curled her lips to grin at me. I guess this felt just as good for her as it did for me.

The first couple of times I moved in and out of her, I could feel her adjust to me, to the feel of me inside of her. On my next movement, I felt Angel let go. Let out her breath. Her movements mirrored mine, and I knew it wouldn't be long before I came.

But first, I had to make her come. Just like I said I would. I knew my mouth with the help of my fingers had already done the job of pushing her over the edge into oblivion. But now my cock had a job to do. I wanted to feel her tighten around me the same as she'd tightened around my fingers.

My hand left Angel's face and travelled down her body to her breasts. I pinched her other nipple, harder than the last time, just to see how much it turned her on. Angel's sex muscles spasmed around my cock and when I moved inside of her, the wetness I'd just caused coated me, and I almost lost my load. I couldn't do that again. I moved my hand farther down her body, brushed my fingertips over her skin to the top of her sex and, when I reached her clit, I rubbed gentle circles until I felt she was close.

'Come for me, Angel. I know you're close,' I breathed out as I looked down into her darker hazel eyes.

'Ohhh my,' Angel breathed back to me, and I knew this would be close.

On the next pump of my hips, I felt Angel fall over the edge of her bliss, and she took me with her. I should've known that would happen. Angel's muscles clamped around me and milked me dry. I should have known there would be too much cum. I filled the condom, and I knew that if I didn't withdraw slowly now, my cum would spill out into her. I didn't know if she used birth control or not, and I wanted to be responsible now that my slate was clean.

I knew she wasn't ready to let go and that I might hurt her a little, but it was better than the alternative.

Normally, I would take things slow, pump my hips a few times as my cock started to soften, but I couldn't do that with Angel. I pushed both of her knees up over her hips and pulled out. I got off the bed and made my way to the bathroom to take care of the mess I had made of myself. I was glad when she didn't follow me. I pulled off the condom and threw it in the bin. I caught my reflection in the mirror, but I couldn't get caught up in what I saw. I knew what I had just done was a move I wasn't proud of, but what else was I supposed to do? I needed to clean myself up and get back to her. Soothe her before shit hit the fan.

I found two washcloths under the sink and ran them under the tap to warm the material. Once they were the temperature I wanted, I quickly cleaned myself up, took the other washcloth with me and left the bathroom to find Angel in the foetal position in the middle of the bed.

'Angel,' I whispered. Her face was wet when I ran my thumb along her cheek. I pushed my fingers into her hair and left my hand there.

'That hurt,' she got out around her sobs. Her words were quiet with a hint of anger.

'I'm sorry, Angel,' I told this incredible woman. 'You milked me dry and then some. I filled the condom, and I was about to fill you, too.' There was a moment's silence between us. 'We've just met. Are you ready for what happens when sex is unprotected?'

There was more silence between us. She must have thought seriously about what I had just said. I brushed my thumb along her cheek again, and no more tears had fallen. I handed Angel the warmed washcloth and she placed it between her legs. I scooped her up and put her on my lap, then pulled the doona and top sheet down and moved both of us under the covers. We laid face to face.

'Angel, I'm sorry I hurt you.'

She silenced me with her finger on my lips.

'You're right. We have just met, and I'm not ready for what unprotected sex will bring.' Angel moved her fingers from my mouth and covered them with her lips. 'What you made me feel was better than I have ever felt before. Even with our abrupt ending.'

'I won't promise it will get better every time because I know you hate promises, so you will just have to believe I'll do my best to always make you feel good. You will always come first, Angel. Always.'

She kissed my lips and that was the end of our conversation. Rolling over, she pushed her back into my chest and snuggled into me. I wrapped my arm around her and held onto her. I loved the way this felt right now. It was the last thing that ran through my thoughts before I fell asleep.

For the first time since Angel and I had spent time together, I woke first. Sex must have worn her out. I filed that piece of information away for later for when I wanted her to stay with me all night. I didn't know what time it was, but had tomorrow even kicked in yet?

I unwrapped myself from around her and got out of bed with a smile on my face. I pulled on shorts and a tee-shirt, grabbed my wallet, phone and keys. I headed for the café in

Robert Street. I wanted to surprise Angel with a coffee. I knew exactly what she liked: latte with a shot of caramel.

But I didn't even make it as far as the café. Lex called. She gave me an update and wanted the go-ahead to pay the pub bills from my account. I answered her and never saw my feet fly out from underneath me. I braced for my fall to the concrete and tried to fight back with the swing of my legs. But nothing prepared me for the boot I received to my face. I fell in and out of consciousness, but that didn't stop the blows my body received.

# Twenty-two

The sweetest melody reached out to me and pulled me back from the blackness I seemed to be lost in. Lyrics I wanted to comprehend but couldn't because they were hummed out next to me. But I understood one word, 'Angel' from the Sarah McLachlan song, and it made me think of my angel. Was she humming that song to me?

I stirred, and the song hung in the air around me. I made the smallest movement and that was when I heard several gasps let out into the silence. I wanted to open my eyes to see what all the commotion was about, but everything hurt way too much. *What the fuck? Where was I? What the hell had happened?*

'Sweetheart.' There was only one person who called me that. She was here with me but was not the person who was cuddled up next to me or the person who had a hold of my hand.

'Mum,' the word was a whisper and even without my eyes open, I knew that voice.

I felt her lean over me and kiss my forehead. I didn't need to see her face to know that she had shed tears recently. Shit must be bad for her to be here. Wherever here happened to be.

'Connor,' my sister whispered, the pain evident in her voice, and I knew she was the one that had a hold of my hand. 'I'm sorry. I know you told me to stay away from your money, but I couldn't help myself,' Lex said through her tears. 'I needed to balance out your investments.'

'Alex. Stop.' The words were nearly too painful to get out. They needed to be loud enough to get her attention, and even then, I had to try to squeeze her hand. 'I'm not mad,' were the almost soundless words that come out.

'Alex.' I knew that voice, too. The deep, rough timbre sent shivers through the room. It wasn't cold, and the man wasn't angry. That was just his voice. My father's voice. He knew how to command the room, a reason he was so damn good at his job. I looked up to my dad, but he left shoes I wasn't sure I knew how to fill, even if I had many lifetimes to live.

At the sound of his voice, I felt Lex let go of my hand, and I knew that my dad had pulled her into his embrace.

'Dad.' The word was muffled, and I knew her head was on his shoulder.

'Mr Black.' Someone new had entered the fold, and I wondered who the new voice wished to speak to.

'Yes,' came the reply. But more than one voice had answered. My brother. Zach was here, too. Why was I surprised by that? The things my brother did would always amaze me. But did he come by choice, or was he forced?

'Of course, you aren't the only male in your family, Connor,' the new female voice stated. As she no doubt took in her fill of the man candy that was the Black family. 'Now that

Connor is awake and you have all seen him, he needs to rest. Everyone needs to leave.'

My mum kissed my forehead again. Lex reached for my hand, closed her fingers over mine and squeezed. If I wasn't where I was, I would have Lex wrapped up in my arms, but it wasn't meant to be. My dad squeezed my shoulder once, then let go. That was okay, Dad. That wasn't painful at all. Lex let go of my hand, and I knew my dad had pulled her away and probably placed her into our mother's arms this time.

'Zach.' I knew he was still in the room. I could feel the moment he stepped closer to me. He didn't touch me, and I was okay with that. We didn't have that kind of relationship. 'You're here?'

'Lex insisted. Says she couldn't stand the thought of you hurt somewhere and not being able to help you.'

'Thank you,' were the only words I could get out. The others had choked on the lump in my throat.

All of a sudden, it was too hard to speak. Silence fell around me and all that could be heard was the sound of shuffled feet as they left my presence.

'Take care, Connor.' The soft words spoken had come from none other than Harley James. Her well wishes would let me know she no longer despised me. Harley's presence wasn't for me, though, it was for Zach, and I would be a fool if I didn't know he needed her for the shit I just couldn't seem to escape, but managed to drag everyone into. But I was working my way through the mess I had created, to come out the other side as a man with simpler needs.

'Someone did a real good number on you.' The female voice from earlier clearly spoke the words into the silence. A silence I couldn't seem to escape. 'But that someone held back.'

'Not someone,' I answered. Little did I know that the silence didn't mean everyone had left. I was unable to open my eyes, and I still didn't know where I was or what had happened, much less who was still here. All I knew was that I was sore, and there was still someone cuddled up next to me.

'Connor!' My dad hadn't quite crossed over the threshold of the exit of where I was, and said, 'You know who did this?'

'If you mean the person who inflicted all this pain I'm feeling.' I heard the beep of a machine give me something that took the tiniest edge off of the agony that coursed through by body. So, I was in hospital. 'Then, yeah, I know.'

'Care to share?' The question was asked quietly, but an answer was demanded. My dad just knew how to get what he wanted. He was a damn good Detective Sergeant, the best interrogator on the force, and why his family never got to see him. But for him to be here, this must be big for him. Maybe I would never understand why he just showed up out of the blue, but being here made sense. I had reached out to inform him of my altercation with Angel's brother and also because I had questions about Angel's DVO.

It hurt to speak. 'The lawyer who worked for me, Paul Christensen. I hired him to help me with all the businesses I owned and made him a rich man. When I sold my businesses one by one, I no longer needed him and told him as much. But Paul thought otherwise. He was pissed I cut him off, only because he thinks I'm starting my next big adventure without him.' I could hear my dad pull something out of his pocket. His phone, a note pad? I wasn't sure, but he made a note either way.

'No,' Lex said, and I knew by the anguish in her voice that she had heard Dad and me talking. Did she know something too?

'Alex.' My dad must have turned around to face her. 'What do you know that you won't tell me?'

Lex didn't respond with any words, only an action that had our father ask her another question. 'Alex, you have a black eye. What did you get messed up in?'

This time, it was me who gasped at the thought of my sister with a black eye. That someone had hurt her, and I missed it. What arsehole didn't look out for his sister? Me. That was who. She hadn't taken her sunglasses off yesterday when I saw her. Was that the reason why?

My gasp was ignored as my sister answered. 'The creep stalked me from the moment we crossed paths a few weeks ago. I don't know how he knew I'm related to Connor, but he did. Maybe he thought he could get to Connor through me. He likes surprise attacks, hence the black eye. We sparred for a few minutes, I kicked out his knee before I had him pinned down and his fingers bent back. I think I broke his hand, Dad. I let him go when Brad arrived, and that's when he made his escape.'

I knew my dad had Lex in his embrace again. 'You did good, Honeybee. You remembered your training. But I will need statements from both of you.' This was a big deal for my dad. He must really want to take Paul down.

'He still got the jump on me, Dad. I want you to take him down hard. Or Connor to kick the shit out of him.' Lex's words brought on a fresh wave of tears that fell not just from her face but mine too. The moisture stung my eyes, and the gentlest touch wiped them away.

'I will, Honeybee,' my dad told my sister. I heard the kiss he left on the top of her head. 'And Connor, don't get any ideas. Let me handle this. Don't go anywhere near Paul.'

I murmured my acquiescence before footsteps retreated away from me.

'I'm sorry, miss.' I felt the body next to me stiffen. Snuggled in next me so comfortably I forgot she was even there. 'He needs rest. That means you have to go.'

'She stays, or I go.' With every effort I had, I said the words and moved my arm around her, and she moved even closer to me and pressed her body next to mine.

'Very well, your woman gets to stay. But on my end-of-shift rounds, if you two aren't anything but asleep, she's out.'

Your woman. These words sounded weird to my ears, but I liked it, and I would like it if Angel really was my woman, if our relationship was that far along.

'Okay,' we said in unison, and then we both couldn't help but let out a snort, which hurt, so I stopped. Angel, though, laughed softly at the expense of my soreness. I couldn't be mad her. Her laughter soothed more of the edges off my discomfort.

# Twenty-three

'Angel,' I whispered. It was the first time I had acknowledged her since I'd heard her sing to me. I felt her next to me, let her warmth cover me like a second blanket, but I couldn't open my eyes and look at her. That shit just hurt way too much.

Into the quietness of my now-vacated room, she asked me. 'How much money makes a man rich?' I realised that Angel and I didn't know each other all that well. She didn't know about my past and the things I'd done back then, as well as recently, not all of it anyway. 'You don't need to work. You could live off what you have?'

'If I did that, then I never would have come back to The Grand and stayed long enough to meet you.' My words were honest. 'It's true, I don't have to work, but I don't want to be the person I was before, and the work I did for Jackie helped with that.'

'Would you have sat at that bar every day until the day I walked in?'

Angel wanted to know if I would chase her, at the end of the day. I would chase her, until the end of time. I know that now. 'Yep,' I told the woman laying right next to me. 'You stirred up something inside of me that night. You were adorable even when you were angry. I've wanted more ever since. Of you. Of the way you make me feel.'

'But I'm just a primary school teacher whose money will never match yours. Why would you want me?'

Did she really think I cared about all the money I had? Or how much she did or didn't have? 'Where does all your money go?' I was curious. I wanted to know why money mattered so much.

'Bills and food. I pay for everything. My brother has his own money but since he moved in with me, he hasn't helped pay any of the bills. I know Lucas pisses his money down the drain at the pub most nights. My brother is up to something. I just haven't figured it out yet.' I wondered how much money Angel was left with at the end of the week.

'Has your brother taken advantage of you the whole time he has lived with you?' I wanted to know how long this had been going on.

'Lucas came to visit twelve months ago. I don't think he is ever going to leave.' There had to be a way to get Angel away from Lucas. I just had to find a way.

'Tell me you're not bothered by the amount of money I have?' If she were bothered by how much I had, I would give it all to her in a heartbeat. I would live off the money I'd earned working for Jackie, and I hoped I would find another job before that money ran out.

Angel didn't speak, there was just a shake of her head I felt on my shoulder. Then I heard, 'I was so excited when I heard I got a posting where I wouldn't be close to my family. I wanted to be able to prove to myself that I could be a young independent woman. My parents worry about me like all parents worry about their children, they check up on me from time to time, and I call them every other week. They encouraged me to apply for this teaching position, so I don't want to believe my parents suggested to Lucas that he check up on me, knowing how domineering he can be, but he showed up out of the blue. I think that if he'd called, I would have told him not to bother coming. I was happy being independent and I love the country lifestyle Mulwala offers, but ever since Lucas showed up and started trying to control my life, then abusing me. I feel like I will never be able to escape him. I know that if I move, he will just follow me, and I like my parents just won't believe me if I told them what's been going on. He could never do wrong in their eyes – their firstborn son. And they're not around to see the bruises. You know, when I first moved into that three-bedroom cottage, it was fully furnished and homely. I was slowly making the place my own. Ever since Lucas moved in, he has smashed everything to pieces in his fits of rage, and I can't afford to replace what he has broken, and if I did, he would just smash that too.'

Her brother really was a meaner son of a bitch than I was and if I ever crossed paths with him again, I would take him out for every time Angel had told me he'd hurt her.

I wanted Angel to know it wouldn't always be like this. She wouldn't always have to live with her brother. But how did I tell her that? Angel didn't know, but when I got out of this hospital bed, things would be different. Once again, I was surrounded by silence as Angel ended that conversation then changed the topic.

'You've got to sleep, baby. That's what the nurse said.' Maybe she didn't want to talk to me anymore.

'No one has ever called me that.' I didn't know why I told Angel that. No one else had ever bothered to call me anything other than Connor. And arsehole didn't count. Maybe I could get use to that term of endearment from her pretty pink lips.

'Okay,' Angel said, and I could hear the disappointment in her voice and for every effort I tried not to be an arsehole, I still was one.

'Say it again,' I said as close as I could to the ear of the woman who chose to crawl up into the place I laid in and stayed next to me.

'Say what?' A coy question. Her disappointment was almost gone from her voice.

'You know.' I held my breath just to hear her say that word again.

'Baby?' This time when she said it, I could hear the smile in her voice. I tried to smile before I let out the breath, I held in.

'You can call me that anytime you want, when it's me and you.' I squeezed the first piece of flesh I could reach, which was her hip.

'Just like you call me Angel?'

Did she not like that I called her Angel? I thought she did.

'What else do you want me to call you?' I was unprepared for what Angel would tell me.

'My name,' she whispered to me.

'Woman,' I huffed. 'Why do you think I call you Angel? I know Mac isn't your name.'

Angel didn't say anything, and I was worried what her opinion was of me calling her Angel? Did she really think I believed Mac to be her Christian name?

I felt Angel move her hand away from my side and that was when I knew I had to offer her some comfort. I moved my arm and felt a tube follow my movement. There was an IV in my hand, which was where my pain relief was being administered. I cupped her face as best I could and brushed my thumb over her jaw.

'Angel!' I couldn't help but give her hip another squeeze.

'Morgan,' she said in my ear. 'Morgan Asher Campbell. That's where Mac comes from.'

'Morgan,' I said as softly as I could, and I liked the way it sounded as it rolled off my tongue. 'Morgan Asher Campbell.' Her whole name sent goose bumps over my body. I was afraid I would never be able to get enough of the woman that lay next to me.

'God,' she breathed out. 'When you say it, it sounds so good. Especially when you say my full name.' Morgan moved slightly. Not sure of what she was doing, she leaned in and pressed her lips to my jaw. She must have found a place that wasn't bruised. I don't know how she knew that was what I needed, but she did, and I loved it. I loved her for it.

'Morgan,' I said again, and I felt her shiver next to me. She liked me saying her name, and I loved the feel of her in my arms. The comfort she gave me by just being her, she was like a protective bubble just for me.

A silence fell around us, but it wasn't uncomfortable. Just when I thought she had fallen asleep and that I might drift off myself, I felt her move and let out a shaky breath. I slid my hand from her jaw into her hair and pulled her closer to me.

'How bad is it?' I couldn't see anything, so I didn't know. All I knew was what I felt, and I felt like shit. My upper body hurt like hell. My face didn't feel much better. I didn't know how many kicks I received or how many punches I took. Everything was sore, and it hurt to move.

'Connor,' her voice was just as shaky as her breath. As I waited for the rest of what she wanted to say. But her words didn't come.

'Angel, if I could open my eyes, I wouldn't need to ask.' I didn't want to have to ask, but for some reason, I wanted to know how much damage that fucker did to me.

'Connor, bad doesn't cover it,' I felt her wriggle around a little, settle then place her hand on my chest.

I removed my hand from Angel's hair and waited patiently for her to continue.

'You have bruises everywhere, dark ones all over you and if you thought my bruises where bad, yours are worse by so much more. Your face is a mess, bruised and bloody, welts and gashes. A thousand times worse than when I clocked you. You can't open your eyes because they are swollen shut. You are here in hospital because of the swelling on your brain and the bruising across your abdomen.'

'I'm sorry,' I whispered into the silence. 'I'm sorry we are here like this.' But inside I was furious I'd let that bastard get the jump on me.

'Shh shh,' Angel hushed as she moved her fingers to my lips, then she rested her hand back on my chest. 'I woke up alone, Connor. You were just gone, and I didn't know what to think. Then your mother showed up to tell me and Jackie's sons that you had been beaten and were in the hospital. They are going to come and see you next time they visit their mother.'

I heard the concern in her voice, and it tore at my heartstrings. I knew I had to ease some of the pain she felt. 'I went to get coffee from the café across the road from the apartment. I remember Lex called me, as she wanted to ask me something pub related. Then she wanted to know what to do. There were bills and the staff that needed to be paid. I gave her the go-ahead to use my money. The office at the pub is a total mess, and it's been two years since a tax return had been filed. Lex was on the phone when I was attacked. I didn't even make it to the café.'

'Oh my God,' Angel breathed out. 'You were gone for so long. I didn't know, I'm sorry.'

'I wanted to surprise you with coffee. Just the way you like it,' I told Morgan. 'Then I was going to kiss that coffee off your lips. We could have laid in bed all morning before we hung out with the Thomas' and wandered around Melbourne.'

'Connor.' I knew Morgan's mind had drifted off to where my lips on her lips would have led by the way my name came out breathless.

'This is not how I thought we would spend our time in Melbourne, Morgan. I thought we could all hang out, visit Jackie while she recovered and see some sights in the after-noons. I never would have gone for coffee if I knew that fucker would be waiting to get the drop on me.'

There was moment when neither of us spoke and before it went on too long, I gave Morgan an out. An option if she really wanted to walk away and never look back or have to worry about me. 'I don't blame you if you want to walk away as my past isn't pretty.' I let my words sink in then said, 'If my past is too much for you, or if I'm more than you can handle, I under-stand.'

I didn't know in this moment if Angel would get up and walk away or not. She sobbed on my shoulder, and I had to tell her words that would make her stay with me. 'I want you next to me for as long as you want to stay by my side. If I am what you want and you don't want to leave, then say so.'

'Baby. You make me feel more special than anyone else in my life. I want to find a way for us to be together even though I will have to go back to work, and you have your recovery ahead of you here in Melbourne.'

'I don't know how long my recovery will take, but I want you to know when I get the 'all clear' from the doctors, I will come for you. In the meantime, I want you to be safe, Morgan.'

'Okay.'

But even hearing those words I didn't fully comprehend how Morgan would keep herself safe or how long it would take for me to recover and for us to finally be together.

I opened up the blanket that was wrapped around me, and I didn't even have to tell Morgan to snuggle in, she just did. When she was comfortable enough next to me, I covered us up, wrapped my arm around her and kissed her forehead.

No more words were spoken. Our breaths evened out. I wasn't sure how long we laid together before we drifted off to sleep. Did she fall asleep first or did I? All I knew was that my woman was by my side. I was grateful for the time she stayed in my arms.

# Twenty-four

My hospital stay lasted a little more than a week. That was how badly I was beaten. My body, from what I could see out of my two still-swollen eyes, was covered in various stages and colours of bruises. A bandage around my torso covered my ribs and the occasional red welt.

I didn't need a mirror to know how bad my face was. I knew. The headaches, the dizziness and the fact I couldn't keep my eyes open let me know I wasn't in good shape. There was also my swollen brain and the bruising around my internal organs. My daily routine consisted of multiple scans and an ice bath. It was exhausting, and by the end I was glad to be taken back to my room and given medication to make me sleep.

The truth of my condition was that it would take a while before my injuries healed and my skin returned to the colour it should be. So even though I was being discharged from hospital, I was swapping hospital walls with four of my own. But at least at home I could slip into the darkness and quietness and recover without the constant interruptions to take my blood pressure or change my drip or replace my morphine vial.

I didn't know what time it was or what day it was for that matter. Only that twice a day I would wake to take the pain medication I'd been sent home with. It made me delirious, a bubble I was comfortable in, and irritable if I wasn't in it. Every day was spent in bed rolling through various stages of just asleep to deep sleep.

Through the darkness in either my room or my mind, I heard whispers as though there were people trying to reach in and pull me out of my delirium. Were they Mum's, Morgan's, Jaime's, Jarryd's, Jason's and Lex's voices I heard? Their words were never loud enough for me to determine who was here.

Maybe I just dreamed the voices in my head, the same as I dreamed Morgan had laid down beside and snuggled in behind me, sending tingles over my skin when she pressed her lips into the column of my neck. I wanted to pull her close to me and wrap her arm around my waist to keep her tucked into me. I didn't want to believe my pain medication made me only dream my angel was comforting me. But when I opened my mouth to whisper, 'Angel', the feeling of her next to me vanished into thin air.

Waking up with Morgan on my mind left me with images of her floating past, and I wanted to sink deep inside her because the one time we had made love was never going to be enough for me.

Wanting Morgan but knowing she wasn't here, I reached for my new phone. I had a need to hear her sweet voice and know that her brother was staying away from her. But Morgan didn't answer. My other option was to text her, and when I opened our message thread, I saw Morgan had texted me a couple of days ago.

*M: I knew you wouldn't hear me whispering goodbye, but I did before I gently kissed your skin.*

Remembering Angel's lips on my skin, I typed out my message to her.

*C: I wanted to believe you really were wrapped up behind me and that I didn't just dream it.*

Morgan surprised me with her immediate response. Whatever she had been in the middle of she couldn't talk to me but managed to sneak off her replies. I couldn't deny how happy this woman made me.

*M: You're awake. How are you feeling? No, baby, you didn't dream it. I snuggled in behind you.*

*C: I'm not feeling as tired now. I'm glad you snuggled in. I know we didn't plan on this, and I'm sorry our break didn't go as planned.*

*M: I'm sorry I'm not there to help you in your recovery. I made friends with your sister, and we have been hanging out with the Thomas'.*

*C: Please tell me you didn't go home to your brother.*

*M: Lex brought me back at the end of my leave. I told her about Lucas, what you did to him, and the DVO. I told your sister about us, and she offered for me to stay with her. I'm so grateful, and I don't ever want to see my brother again.*

My sister was an amazing woman, and I had to tell her that next time I saw her.

*C: I'm happy you're safe.*

*M: I know you'll want to rush your recovery to get back to me, but I'm okay here with Lex. She has lent me her car and apart from work, I won't go anywhere alone.*

*C: When the doctors give me the 'all clear', I want to find you curled up and sleeping in my bed.*

*M: I miss you and can't wait until your arms are around me.*

*C: I miss you too, Angel.*

*M: I have to go. I'll message you later.*

Morgan missed me and wanted my arms around her and that's right where I wanted to be. But while I was in Melbourne recovering and Morgan was in Mulwala teaching, I would just have to fantasise that my Angel was here next to me. I let my thoughts of Morgan drift away and would wait for her to message me later.

But as I lay here staring up at the ceiling, I wondered how much time had passed. How long had I been in my apartment rolling through my various stages of sleep? Had another week passed? All I knew was that I didn't feel as sleepy as I did when I was in hospital. I was staying awake for longer now, but I just hadn't felt like venturing out of bed yet. I knew I would have to if I wanted to start my recovery.

So, I took stock of my life. I had a job I had been fired from, no car, a business I'd kept secret and hadn't sold because I co-owned it with my brother and had kept it separate from all my other businesses. I had more money than I knew what to do with, a body that needed to heal and an attitude that was souring, but I didn't want it to rule the rest of my life. Because deep down, I knew I was better than this.

I needed to get up and get out of bed, that much was a given. I needed to figure out what I wanted, make a plan and go after it. And it all needed to start in this moment. I sat up slowly, swung my legs over the bed and stood up. I did everything in baby steps because I was still hurt and in some places it hurt like hell. But the more I moved the less stiff I became.

For the first time since my mother had let me into this place, I opened all the blinds and windows. This oasis needed fresh air and sunshine, and it flooded in to rid the darkness and stench of me that had overtaken this two-bedroom apartment. I stood in the sunshine and fresh air of the last window I opened. In the master bedroom I soaked it all in, letting the sunshine warm my face and the fresh air fill my lungs.

Now, I needed to get out, out of this apartment and my own head. I needed to move the muscles of my body and burn off the nervous energy Melbourne always gave me. I could feel it building inside. Before I started pacing my apartment, I pulled on clothes that were easy to get into and would be comfortable to move in. I found socks, shoved my feet into my runners and tied the laces. I grabbed my phone and a holder I could wrap around my arm.

I didn't want to get lost in the music. I wanted to be fully aware of who and what was around me. No one would ever sneak up on me again. No one would ever get the chance to kick my feet out from underneath me. Next time, I would be ready. Next time I would give myself the chance to fight back.

I stood at the door and remembered this was my new phone. There was no way it was set up the way that I liked it. For someone who'd spent over a week sleeping, I was surprised my phone was on and charged. I opened my music app. Some-one had had enough time to play around and make me more than one playlist. I chose one at a level that wasn't too loud. Did Morgan, Lex, Jarryd and Jason all take their turns to create a playlist for me?

I was ready to head off on what I hoped would clear my head and help me regain some of the fitness I'd started to see from not having a car. My only option to get to and from The

Grand was to walk. The moment I stepped out and closed the door, I knew I had forgotten to grab my apartment key.

That would have to be something I dealt with later. Right now, I needed to move. I didn't know how to describe the way I felt. All I knew was that I couldn't just stand here. I rocked on the soles of my feet. Once. Twice. Then, I put one foot in front of the other. I walked down the stairs, then out on to the street, and before I knew it, I was settled into an easy walking pace where it wasn't too hard to breathe. My broken ribs still needed to heal, but weren't in this moment causing me too much trouble.

I didn't know this area very well, so I didn't know where to go and didn't want to stop and look at a map. I found a path that would lead me to the Yarra River. When I crossed the bridge to the parkland on the other side, I knew it was time to turn around and head back to my apartment.

I was a block away from my place when my phone rang. I pulled my phone out of its holder, checked the number, grinned and answered.

'If you are where I think you are, please wait. I'm on my way.' I hung up, tucked my phone into its holder and pushed my luck. I picked up my walking pace as I crossed the street at the lights. As I reached the top of the stairs, the person who stood in my doorway stared me down. I must say, I may have even pissed her off. Slightly.

I could tell by the look on her face that she wasn't impressed that I'd hung up on her. But the concern melted from her face the closer I got. She could tell something had happened to cause the change she saw. I wasn't laid out flat, asleep and delirious. But rather upright, sweaty and outside my apartment.

I leaned in and kissed her cheek. 'I'm sorry I hung up.' I still needed to catch my breath. 'I left my keys inside, and I didn't want to miss you.'

'Jesus, Connor, have you lost your mind? Why did you leave the apartment?' My worried mother put her hand on her hip. I knew that tell. It confirmed that she wasn't impressed. 'What happened?'

'Mum, I'm fine.' I took a couple more breaths, I may have slightly overdone it trying to catch my mother. But I needed to reassure her I was okay. 'I might be a little sore later, but it feels good to be out of bed.' The words I told her were true. But nothing got passed her. She knew something wasn't quite right.

'Connor,' Eva Black all but scolded me.

'Can we go inside?' I said to the woman who no one could get anything past. 'I need a bottle of water.'

'Okay.' She moved aside to let me in. As soon as the door closed, she pounced. 'Connor Shane Black!'

'Mum,' I said as I moved to the kitchen for the bottle of water, which I downed in one go.

'I've checked on you every morning, Connor, for the last ten days. Every day you were sound asleep.'

'Well, not today,' I muttered to myself as I moved passed her and headed towards my bedroom. I knew my medication made me lose track of time. I had lost ten days, and how many days had I lost from my stay in hospital? A week?

I didn't have to turn around to see the look Eva Black gave me. I would always be the cause of her worry. I didn't want the first person I had seen in over a week to be the person that copped the brunt of the bullshit inside my head. But my mother was the best person to handle the shit I needed to get out. I just didn't want to admit that to her.

I closed my bathroom door. I needed a minute. I stepped out of my sweaty clothes and let my frustrated breath go in a huff as my hands landed on the edge of the basin. I stared at myself in the mirror, taking in all the bruises I could still see. There were still various stages of bruising, still red, purple, black and yellow all over me.

But I no longer needed to sleep for long periods, a sign I was getting better. My body was slowly improving. My mental health, I needed to work on that. But I couldn't do that unless I showered first. A shower would help to wash off the smell of sweat and the grime that had covered me in the last ten days. I needed a change of clothes, ones I could lounge around in if I were going to lay my bullshit out in front of my mother, before I took my medication and went back to bed.

It wouldn't have mattered how long I took. I knew when I left my bedroom that my mother would still be here. What surprised me was that she had made eggs, bacon and hash browns for breakfast and cappuccinos from the coffee machine she insisted be purchased for all of our apartments. She would do anything to make me talk, and right now, the way to get what she wanted was definitely through my stomach.

The smell of breakfast hit me as soon as I opened the bathroom door. Like a moth drawn to the flame, my nose took me closer to the kitchen and to what my mother had made. I reached in to steal the bacon off the plate she had just dished up when I got a slap on my hand.

'Talk to me,' she said with her eyebrows drawn together. She waved her hand around the plate. 'Then you get to have some of this.'

'Today was the first morning my alarm went off that I didn't automatically reach for my pain meds. After texting

Morgan, I felt this ball of energy around me that made me want to punch something. I decided to get out of the house,' I admitted to my mother, but really, I needed to say it out loud for my own benefit. Then I could do something about the way I now felt.

'Why? What happened?' she asked, and I shrugged like I didn't know what had changed. But nothing got past Eva Black, not when she was in psychologist mode, which I had to admit she didn't really know how to turn off.

'I locked myself out. The moment I closed the door behind me, I knew the keys were still inside.' My mum took the plate she'd dished up in one hand and the coffee she had made in the other. She made her way over to my square dining table. We sat down opposite each other, and she handed me the coffee then the plate. 'It felt different being stuck outside. It left me no choice but to walk or be overcome with fear.'

'Connor, what put you in hospital, what you experienced, was a traumatic event. Some things will feel different from now on. What you do when things feel different will determine whether you sink or swim.'

I dug into the food she placed in front of me and listened to what she had to say. She would have wise words to part with. My job was to listen and consider her advice.

'What you experienced before your walk was no doubt a panic attack, and it's normal to have them after what you've been through. But if you let them control you, you will spiral out of control and fall down the rabbit hole quicker than you ever thought possible.'

'What do you suggest I do about the racing heart and the nervousness?' I asked around the last mouthful of food.

'I can prescribe you medication. But my recommendation to you is to familiarise yourself with your training. How long has it been since you've been to a self-defence class?'

The words just rolled off her tongue so easily, and I wanted to argue that I didn't need medication or to remember the self-defence I had learnt alongside Lex at our mother's directive when Lex had moved to Melbourne. But Eva knew something I didn't. It was the sole reason as to why she was here today.

'I saw the bruises. You are not invincible, Connor.'

'I know.' I caught my mother turn her head, and was that a tear I saw slide down her face?

'Connor, sweetheart, no mother should have the wits scared out of her, and that's exactly what happened when I saw you in that hospital bed.' There was a moment of silence while she regained her composure. 'You know the classes teach you how to defend yourself, that much is obvious, but the classes teach you more than self-defence and you know this. You learn control. Over your breathing, your anger, and even your fear.' Another silence. 'When you have control, you will feel so much better. And you won't wake up wanting to punch something, that I can guarantee.'

I didn't get to respond to her. She leaned in to kiss my cheek, then she was out of her seat and at the apartment door before I had processed fully what she had said. It was a lot to think about, but I knew she was right. I needed a refresher in self-defence, for better control over my breath, my moods, my anger, my emotions and the need to not be a heartless son of a bitch.

# Twenty-five

My stay in Melbourne would last until I received the 'all clear' from the doctors at the hospital. My recovery though, according to the paperwork the hospital sent me home with now that I was capable of reading, depended on me attending outpatient appointments, plenty of rest and gentle exercise. Which I unintentionally started when I locked myself out two days ago.

What better way to fill my time than to organise the things I needed in my life: a truck with a particular rumble and a piece of paradise I could call home in Mulwala. Time to start a to-do list. But first I needed to check in with my father and find out if there was any news on the prick who'd attacked me. My father's response was that Paul had gone quiet and that I still needed to fill out an incident report. I added catching up with Preston Black to my to-do list.

Both Brock and Jaime had kept me up to date with what was happening at The Grand Hotel. Jaime had gone as far as setting up a group message with his brothers, mother, Alex and myself. Not only was I kept up to date with what was happening at the bar, the Thomas boys also used the group message to keep me updated on their mother's condition.

Jaime had spent three weeks checking on his mother and making sure his brothers were okay, before he headed back to Mulwala to overhaul both the lunch and dinner menus. Jaime wanted his mother's transition back to work to be seamless, but it all depended on whether Jackie was happy to let him continue running the dining room, because Jackie still needed someone other than Jarryd behind the bar, and Jason was too young.

After checking I had no other unread messages, I moved on to add my money to my to-do list. I couldn't purchase any big-ticket items until I sorted what I was going to do with the money I had made from the sale of all my businesses, now that my debts were paid off. That meant I had to come clean. I had to tell my siblings what I'd done.

I'd told Zach and Lex I'd sold them all, my array of businesses. But I couldn't bring myself to sell The Groove, my first joint venture. The Groove was my rainy-day venture, the one I kept separate from all of my other businesses.

Before purchasing The Groove, I'd worked my way up through an event-planning business, Bright, before I eventually purchased it. Then I acquired more businesses to expand Bright that I was left short on capital. When The Groove came on the market, I had needed Zach's help. He had given me the money for the bar in Fitzroy, but opted to be a silent partner because he knew I was a fool and would never listen to any of his advice. The Groove was the one business Paul didn't know about because I had kept it separate from all of my other businesses. So, I didn't sell The Groove.

Now that I was cleaning up my image, I needed to extend it to my business. My rainy-day moment was here, my only income. It was time to put into practice everything I had learnt. Everything Jackie had taught me, to see if I really did have what it took to successfully run my own business. A clean business without the shady deals on the side. Prove to myself that I could be worthy of Morgan and be able to shower her in the gifts she deserved.

Morgan. My woman. My angel. Thoughts of her on her knees with her lips around me and me cursing up a storm trying not to cum. Because if she really were here, I wanted to pick her up, lay her down, kiss every inch of her perfect skin and make love to her. But Morgan wasn't here, so I reached down and cupped my balls as they swelled and my cock stiffened. I stroked myself slowly at first as images of Angel filled my mind and my veins with sensations that would bring me to my release. I knew she couldn't hear me, but I still panted out the name I had called her that very first day.

Cleaning myself up, I let the hot water run down my body. I lathered body wash, rinsed and dried off. I changed the bandage around my ribs and got ready to make a presence at the business I owned. I pulled on briefs, then dark blue jeans. I was about to rummage through my clothes to find a half decent tee-shirt to wear when I heard my phone ring.

'You want to tell me why you are still paying bills at The Groove?' As soon as I answered, this was the barrage I got from Lex. 'You told me you sold everything?'

'I thought I told you to leave the money alone, Alex.' I used my sister's given name because I knew it pissed her off. She deserved it, too. I had already told her to leave well enough alone.

'Argh, Connor. You know I can't help myself,' my sister snapped at me. 'Do you know how much that place has lost recently?'

The realisation that I had lost money, no matter how big or small, nearly made me blow a gasket. The business that was supposed to be my backup plan wasn't meant to go backwards and lose money. But it was my own fault as I hadn't watched The Groove like a hawk, like I was supposed to. I hadn't paid enough interest to what was happening from month to month. Now I knew I needed to pay more attention.

I opened my mouth to speak, but nothing came out. I fought for control of the red I saw. I wouldn't let hearing that I'd lost money get the better of me. I took a deep breath in, counted to five and then let it out. I took another breath in, counted to five again and I knew it was audible. I knew Lex had heard me. My exhale came out ragged. The next words out of her mouth were softer.

'You can fix this, Connor.' Lex's words were an encouragement.

'I can fix this.' Then, I repeated the same words a few more times in my head. 'And I start tonight.' I didn't tell Lex that my plan was to go in before The Groove opened and tell the staff I planned to close temporarily.

'I'll meet you there.' I didn't bother to argue with her. She already knew all about my money. Now she could understand about the one business I still owned too. 'And Connor,' Lex added, 'you need to call Zach. He has a right to know that you didn't sell and that he's been losing money too.'

Lex's words hit me like a slap in the face. I couldn't deny I hadn't consulted Zach at any stage on any of the decisions over the years that needed to be made at The Groove. I had accepted his money without further thought and now that I needed to turn things around, Zach's assistance would be more than valuable. I just hoped he was willing to help me.

I thanked Lex and hung up.

I found the tee-shirt I wanted to wear and slipped it on as I contemplated what to tell Zach about The Groove. I hesitated, but then I found Zach's number in my phone and called him.

When he answered my call, we exchanged hellos, and Zach asked how I was doing since my attack. Then I quickly spilled what I had called to tell him. 'Zach, I didn't sell The Groove. With your help and Alex brought in as a co-owner, I want the business to be just like Little Beats is. Successful.'

'I know you didn't sell.'

'How?'

'The paperwork I signed made no mention of The Groove, and the money you put in my account wasn't enough for what you would get for a karaoke bar in Melbourne.'

My brother was right. The Groove, even Zach's share, would be worth three times as much I had already given him.

'Connor,' my brother interrupted my thoughts. 'A successful business doesn't happen overnight, and it's a big job to pull that off.'

'If you want out, I understand. I have the money to give you if you want more than your share.' I wanted my brother to know he had an option. Of out, if he wanted it. I would understand, as I hadn't been honest.

'Where are you?' I was surprised that Zach had asked that question.

'On my way to The Groove.'

'I will meet you there. I'm here to check on Little Beats.'

I was shocked by Zach's words. By the way he spoke to me, he wasn't angry. It sounded like he wanted to help. I would take any support I could get, especially from my brother. His expertise was priceless. He was already a successful businessman.

I pulled on socks and boots and set out on foot for The Groove. I should have known that I wouldn't have to wait for Lex. I didn't mention a time to meet, but it was no wonder she was here right as the doors were about to open.

'Connor,' Lex said as she approached me. 'I thought you wanted a fresh start?' My sister got straight to the point, skipping the pleasantries.

'Hello Alex,' I said as I wrapped her up in my hug. I knew she hated it when people called her Alex. But she skipped the pleasantries, so I got to call her Alex. 'And I'm good, thanks for asking. How's Morgan?'

'Okay. Hello.' Lex tried to wriggle out of my embrace, but she didn't get out of my embrace that easily. 'It's good to see you're out of bed. Morgan is good. She misses you. Her brother is an even bigger arsehole than you, and boy is he pissed at you for knocking him out cold. I had the pleasure of meeting him the day he smashed Morgan's phone. I may have broken the bastard's wrist for violating his DVO.'

'Jesus, Lex. Please tell me you informed dad of your little run in with Lucas Campbell.' My sister was never going to hold back now that she had been attacked.

'Dad knows,' Lex huffed out.

'I hope you called the police to tell them the DVO had been violated?'

My sister raised our trademark one eyebrow at me. 'Of course I did,' she scoffed at me, and I knew she didn't like me questioning her.

'Did you replace Morgan's phone?' I pulled my phone out to tell Morgan I would call her later. There was a rushing of blood in my veins and a need to know my Angel was okay.

My sister nodded, smirked, then whispered her tease. 'You must be in love, because man you have it bad for that woman.'

Lex was right, I did have it bad, and yes, what I felt was love but I wasn't confessing anything to anyone until I'd told Morgan those three little words. There was no denying I missed my woman and her curled up next to me with her arm around me.

I gave Lex one of my shit-eating smirks. 'Thank you.' Now our banter was over, I held my sister at arm's length, my tone serious as I continued. 'I'm grateful for everything you have done for me, especially offering Morgan to stay with you. I appreciate it.'

Was that a tear I could see in Lex's eye? I wasn't sure and there was no way I was about to call her out on it. She would probably kick my arse for it. But I knew she needed to hear my words.

Before I let go of Lex, I dropped my bombshell on her. 'I couldn't bring myself to sell The Groove. It's the first business Zach ever loaned me money for, and although he's been a silent partner, I want to make it work.'

'Jesus, Connor. Zach will be pissed,' Lex said as we locked eyes.

'We'll find out soon enough, I guess.'

She was surprised by my words.

'You called Zach?' Did she really think I was chicken shit?

'He said he would meet me here. He was checking on Little Beats.'

As I took a step back, I noticed my sister had brought company.

'You have a shadow,' I said loud enough for only Lex to hear me.

'Yeah, for three weeks now no thanks to you.'

I knew my sister was only yanking my chain.

'What? Wait? What do you mean me?' Maybe my sister was serious.

'Paul. I can't believe you two worked together. He's more ruthless than you.'

'I didn't know Paul had mean streak a mile wide otherwise he never would have been my confidant. How did you ever get tangled up with him?' I was curious as to why Lex would ever hang out with someone like him.

'We ran into each other one afternoon and couple of times after that. Then his behaviour became stalkerish, and he would follow me home after drinks on Friday nights. After Paul's surprise attack left me with a black eye and your stay in hospital, Brad has kept his eye on me. The two of us have hung out a little bit.' Lex let out an exasperated breath.

'Don't tell me you don't enjoy Brad's company.' I pushed Lex's buttons, the same as she pushed mine a moment ago. I took in Lex's face and her frustration. I could see she liked him, even if she never would admit it to me. 'You two look good together.'

Lex let out an exasperated breath and whacked me with her forearm into my side. I may have gone a little too far with my tease. No way was I about to double over in pain or tell her that she just got me in the same ribs I'd been kicked in. My body was still sore more than three weeks after I had been beaten.

'Jesus, Lex.' I swallowed down my pain.

'Can we just go inside?' Lex turned to make her way inside.

'Zach will be here soon,' I told Lex and she turned back to look at me. 'We wait for Zach. What I have planned won't work without him.'

Lex raised her eyebrow at me, giving her silent 'really'. So, I matched her raised eyebrow and nodded my head.

'Would you rather I left him in the dark about this?' I pointed to the neon sign that lit up the name of the business we stood out the front of.

'Point taken.'

'The sooner Zach knows about my plans for The Groove, the less likely he is to be pissed with me. If there is one thing I've learnt, it's that I have to be truthful and do things honestly and by the book.'

'Okay. It was the right thing to do. To let Zach know,' Lex confessed.

When Zach arrived, he shook hands with Lex's shadow, and I introduced myself to Brad. 'I'm Connor by the way,' I said as I stuck my hand out for Brad to shake. He did, as I continued, 'Sorry, Lex here was rude and didn't introduce us.'

Lex shot me her death stare as Brad replied. 'Lex wants to keep me a secret but it's a bit hard when I know half the family anyway.' Brad knew Lex and Zach, but I was out of the loop as to why. Would anyone care to fill me in? Or would I have to work that one out on my own?

'And now you know another family member.' Lex whacked Brad same as she did to me, only Brad got hit across his chest and not the ribs like me. 'Brad's a lawyer at his dad's firm and he's been helping Harley with her family trust and her dad's estate.'

I appreciated my sister for filling me in.

Lex turned to head towards the entrance of The Groove, but Brad had caught her arm and pulled her back to him. He whispered something in her ear, then let her go. I stood by what I said, they did look good together.

'What's the plan?' Zach faced both Lex and me.

'Well hello to you too.' Lex and I said in unison as we both bear hugged our brother.

'Okay. Okay. Hello. Hello. You look good, Connor. Thought you might have been bullshitting me on the phone.' Zach told me, and both Lex and I let go.

My bruising had almost gone, but my ribs would most likely take the longest to heal. My next scans at the hospital would give me a better indication of the residual minimal swelling on my brain and my internal injuries.

'Now that we're all here and you can see I'm getting better, we can go inside and tell the staff our plans,' I told Zach, Lex and Brad.

'And what plans are they?' Zach asked. The guy did have a right to know what those plans were.

'That the three of us will co-own The Groove, and we are about to take this club in a new direction. A classy one, and the staff can either get on board or go their separate ways.'

'What do you mean, the three of us?' Lex asked like she wasn't sure what just happened.

'I want you brought in as a partner, Lex, and I don't want you as a silent partner anymore either, Zach. I want us to do this together.'

'I'll draw up some papers if you would like to make it official,' Brad said out of the blue, and we all turned to look at him. 'That's what lawyers do,' Brad deadpanned.

Maybe I could reach out to Brad about the property I wanted to purchase?

'Well, I guess that's a start,' Zach threw out. He smirked. I think he liked the idea that I would be held more accountable for what happened at The Groove.

'Like you said, it's a big job and it won't happen overnight. So, it's best that we get to it.'

Turning on my heel, I walked towards the front doors and entered The Groove.

It wasn't easy to tell the staff that the club they worked at was about to be rebranded into a reputable establishment. That it was going to be more than a little classy. Some laughed, walked out, and didn't look back. Some stayed to hear what I had to say and still walked away. In the end, there were only four people left. Us. None of The Groove staff wanted to stay on board.

So here I was, on a stool in my own bar, about to drown a few of my sorrows in a couple of straight bourbons I knew I would regret in the morning, given the pain medication I was weaning off. But right now, I wanted to believe that I knew what I was doing. Not just with this club, but with my family too, and that I could be a man they could be proud of, especially Morgan.

# Twenty-six

I cursed myself for the way I felt, knowing I shouldn't have mixed alcohol with my pain medication. I woke to a sound that reverberated from the front door to the jack hammer in my head. I stumbled my way off my bed, glad my body was still covered in some sort of clothing to check the peep hole.

I opened my door to a full bombardment from Jason. 'You brought us down here to be closer to my mum. I thought we were going to hang out, but you ended up in hospital just like her.'

I reached out and put my hand on Jason's shoulder. 'I know these last couple of weeks haven't turned out the way we planned. But now I'm not as tired and am feeling better, I thought we could hang out.'

'We visited you, and Jaime did as well,' Jason informed me as he and Jarryd walked past me to sit on my lounge. 'Not just in hospital either. Your mum gave us key to come in and check on you. Morgan, Jaime, Jarryd and I, we took turns to set up your new phone. Lex helped too. We all made playlists for you while we told you about our day. And if you haven't checked your photos, you should.'

The music I knew about. The photos I didn't. But I would check them later. There were things I needed to do first.

'How's your mother?' I asked them.

'She's had her surgery now,' Jarryd told me.

'She's tired all the time and asleep most of the time we visit.' Jason huffed. It was evident he wasn't used to not being able to interact with his mother. 'One of the nurses suggested we read to Mum, so Jarryd and I take it in turns. Mostly it's whatever novel we are in the middle of reading. Jarryd's reading crime, and I'm reading a young adult adventure novel.'

'I guarantee you,' I looked at Jason, 'that your mum loves that you visit to read to her even on the days she is sleeping. She needs her rest too, to make a full recovery back to the mother you know her to be.' I looked at both Jarryd and Jason this time. 'You two and Jaime will have to help your mother more than ever now. At home and at the pub.'

I could see both young men were deep in thought. I liked that I had made them think about the need to step up for their mother.

'What about you?' they asked at the same time.

'Me?'

'Do you live here now?'

'This apartment is a gift, but I don't live here. It's true I can stay here, but I don't want to.' There was a property I had my eye on and needed to follow up on to see if it was still available.

'What about the pub? You could stay there.'

Did Jason really think that was a good idea? I surely hoped not.

'You both know I can't live there. I don't work for your mother anymore. Whether Jackie trusts me or not, I'm sure she doesn't want me hanging around.'

'Why not?' Both Jarryd and Jason protested.

'She may have plans to let Jaime stay there now he's back.'

'So, what now?' Jarryd knew there was more to this conversation, and he wanted to know what I was yet to tell them.

'I look for somewhere to live, a place to settle down.' To continue my clean slate, but I didn't say that.

'Where?' two voices asked.

'The same place you guys call home. Mulwala.' What I didn't tell them was that my decision was made not only because of them, or that my brother lived there, but wholly because there was one hazel-eyed beauty who lived there and had completely stolen my heart. Thinking about the angel I could never take my eyes off made me miss her all that much more. I needed to text Morgan same as I had the last couple of days. Maybe I could call her later.

Both Thomas boys jumped up and hurled themselves at me, excited at the news I had told them. I was thankful they didn't squeeze me too tight with their bear hug.

'I know my mum said she didn't want you around the pub, but she will come around.' The words Jarryd told me made me think he was right. But I didn't want to get my hopes up.

Maybe Jarryd was right, maybe he wasn't. Maybe he knew something I didn't. I was told to stay away, so that was what I would do. But that didn't mean that Jaime, when he was in Melbourne, Jarryd, Jason and I couldn't hang out.

My call to Morgan was brief, as she was having lunch and couldn't talk for long. It was a relief to hear that although she was a little shaken up after her run-in with her brother, that she was okay. I was going to kill her brother the next time I saw him, so I just hoped the law got to him first. I hated that I wasn't there to protect Morgan. Soon, I told myself, we could be together, and Angel would always be safe.

For two weeks Jarryd, Jason and I divided our time between the items on the to-do list I had made and visiting their mother. Occasionally I stayed with them while they talked to her, and the other times I had my own outpatient appointments to attend.

Most nights I went to check on The Groove, the bar I now equally co-owned with my siblings, thanks to the contract Brad Waters had drawn up for us. The Groove had new staff because Zach had advertised and hired the right staff. Andy assisted with whom to hire for security, for the front doors and inside the bar. Lex added The Groove to her ever-growing list of books that she did outside of her fulltime job. While it was my job to make sure the staff got along and the customers were happy.

But mostly I wanted to see if any shady deals were being done. With none done, thanks to the staff Zach hired, my employees didn't need me to watch over them like a hawk. Everyone was quite capable. I couldn't help myself. I missed the work I did for Jackie at The Grand. I knew by the time I spent with the staff at The Groove, even when I wasn't here, the business would still run smoothly. All I would have to do was drive down once every couple of months to check that everything was okay. Same as what Zach did with Little Beats.

## Black Eye

At the top of my to do list was the contract for the property I wanted to purchase, the water tower property. I just needed someone to look at the contract. A lawyer, someone I could trust more than the last lawyer I hired. My sister's boyfriend, though I think they might not be there just yet, drew up the contracts for The Groove. It was worth a second opinion on a property I wouldn't see until the day I packed up my arse here and drove to Mulwala to live in it.

I knew the property needed to be renovated, so I was happy to put in a reasonable offer, and Brad's advice would tell me if the property was worth the money I would put in. With Brad's research and professional opinion, I hoped the property I was about to buy wasn't a money pit. I signed the contract and organised to pay the deposit when both Brad and Brock had told me the property was good.

Now that I had the water tower property sorted, I could move on to the next item on my to-do list – my mode of transport. It needed to be black inside and out and it needed to have a particular rumble. One I would pay handsomely for.

Another item I wanted to get off my list: the perfect set of rings. Two wedding bands and an exquisite diamond ring. I wasn't in a hurry, as there was no need to rush to get married. There was a process to relationships, and I hadn't even told Morgan that I loved her. I just knew that Morgan was it for me and wanted the diamond ring for the when moment was just right.

I opened my phone and scrolled through the photos. Everyone who'd had had access to my phone over the last three weeks had taken selfies. My favourite ones were of Morgan when she had grinned cheekily and pulled faces at the camera. The rest of the photos made me laugh. Taking my own selfie, I sent it to Morgan along with a text.

C: *I miss you every single day, Angel.*

M: *Thank you for the photo, baby. Your smiling face is exactly what I needed to see today. I can't wait until I'm tangled up in the sheets with to you.*

Reading Morgan's words made me instantly so hard that I almost typed out 'I love you'. I adjusted myself instead before I cupped my balls and stroked my length. My balls weren't quite blue, but they would be if I didn't get to make love to Morgan soon.

C: *I get better every day, and I can't wait to press my lips to your skin.*

M: *I like the sound of that.*

Messaging Morgan was the best part of my day. I wanted Angel in my life and my arms around her like the lovesick fool that I was. I didn't ever want to let go of how this woman made me feel.

Jarryd and Jason helped me with all the items on my list, even when it came to cleaning out my storage unit, and what I should pack to take with me to Mulwala, what I should keep here in Melbourne and what I should send to charity and landfill. I needed what was left in my storage unit to be able to fit inside the U-Haul trailer I was going to hire and the back of my truck.

Five weeks after I had been attacked, I had been given the 'all clear' from my doctors at the hospital. As an outpatient, there were many appointments I was required to attend where I spoke with my rehab team about my headaches, pain management and muscle stiffness. My hospital visits weren't complete without a whole-body scan to check the swelling on my brain and bruising around my internal injuries.

I texted Lex, hoping it would be okay for me to continue staying at her house while I renovated mine. She replied with yes. I texted Morgan to tell her I had been given the 'all clear' by the hospital. I wanted her to know I was on my way north to her.

# Twenty-seven

The day after receiving my medical clearance, I pulled into Mulwala with my rented U-Haul hooked up to my kitted-out black Ford Raptor, complete with the personalised plates CSB. And I breathed my first real, uncomplicated breath. I knew this little country town was where I wanted to be.

My whole life was packed into either the back of my truck or in the trailer. I had made my decision. I put all of this into motion, cleared out my storage unit in Melbourne of all my belongings, filled my apartment with some of the things I had stored and packed the rest to bring them with me. With a clean bill of health from my doctor five weeks after being attacked, I got behind the wheel of my truck and headed in the direction of this riverside country town.

My life had changed, I had changed, and I didn't need any-thing Melbourne had to offer anymore. The business I shared ownership with my siblings was now good, doing better than I had ever expected, and I was happy to watch over from afar. The bar had a great manager that the three of us trusted, which made things easier. But this little country town was where I wanted my future to be.

Wanting more than anything to kiss Morgan and hold her in my arms, I pulled up outside my sister's house and opened the driver's side door. I heard the sweetest of sounds and acoustic guitars. Like a bull to a red flag, I beelined down the side of the house to see who was singing. Two of the voices I could pick out anywhere, Lex and Harley. The third made me smile. I had heard that voice hum two lines of song as I'd laid in a hospital bed. Morgan. The fourth voice surprised me as it came from Shea, the woman who'd sold me Morgan's clothes.

I wanted to pull Angel into my arms kiss her senseless and leave her breathless before I threw her over my shoulder and stole her away to do more than just have her in my arms. But I knew that was a barbaric move and that Morgan was enjoying her time hanging out with her friends. So, I stood out of sight and listened as they all sang Kelsea Ballerini's 'Yeah Boy'.

I pulled away from Lex's house to make my way to my recently acquired property. I needed to unhitch my U-Haul trailer and unpack the back of my truck. While in recovery, I purchased the property I had expressed an interest in. It had taken a while to get back to the estate agent after my stay in hospital, but once I started the ball rolling on purchasing the fixer upper, I could only dream of the day I pulled into the driveway.

Today would be the first day I got to have a really good look around the property I had bought sight unseen but with a little help from Brock, as well as Brad, who'd helped with the building inspection. I knew just how much work needed to be done and would need Brock's help to make both the homestead and bungalow on the property liveable spaces. The homestead needed a complete renovation. The bungalow was an empty shell. Both had plenty of potential.

The plan was to one day have a studio in half of the bungalow where I could solely work on my acoustic sound, and maybe I could get Morgan to sing with me or Lex or maybe even Harley if she'd work with me. The other half of this bungalow would eventually be a temporary home for Morgan and me while our homestead was renovated.

While I was grateful to Lex for allowing me to continue to stay at her house, our old childhood home, I was looking forward to my own space, to working on what needed to be done around my property.

The moment I pulled my truck up to the double garage of my house, my phone buzzed with an incoming text. From Zach.

*Z: Lex told me you would be in town today. Any chance you could help me out with this local talent event I've got planned? I think you might owe me.*

*C: I just need to park the trailer. I can meet you at Black's.*

*Z: So, you live here now?*

*C: You could say I'm new to town.*

*Z: Good. I have an open spot in the event. I'll put you down. You can fill in.*

*C: Guess I don't have a choice in the matter?*

*Z: I know all about the songs you and Lex have challenged each other with. I'm sure you could find a couple of those songs to play.*

*C: I may be a little rusty, but if you need me to play, I guess I can fill in.*

*Z: You don't want to let your little brother down, do you?*

*C: Never.*

Before I could help Zach, I had to unload my things from my truck. I didn't want to leave them to get stolen when I didn't know how long I would be at Black's Bar and Grill for. I used the remote on my keys and watched as the double garage door rolled upwards. It was the only safe place on this property to use as storage. Once my truck was empty, I made sure my overnight bag and acoustic guitar were on the back seat. Then I headed towards my brother's business.

When I got to Black's Bar and Grill, I saw Zach at the concierge desk. His back was to me, and I hoped I hadn't made him wait too long for me. As the double glass doors opened, I felt the air conditioner hit me. Zach turned around ready to tell me, I was sure, that Black's wasn't open and that I would need to come back when they were, when he recognised it was me. He moved towards me and when he reached me, he offered his hand to shake. I took it.

'How's the recovery going?' My brother skipped asking how I was, asking instead if I was up to helping him out.

'The ribs are still a little sore. Might not be able to lift anything too heavy. Otherwise, I should be okay. You just want me to fill a spot this afternoon to sing?' I knew when my brother asked me to meet him here that he needed my expertise. I didn't mind, and I was ready to do an honest afternoon's work.

'Actually, I could use your help. One of my guys has called in sick, and I need the bars stocked. I've managed to get a replacement for when the event is on. But that's too late to get both bars filled.' The conversation between us flowed better now than it ever had in the past. Better now that he wasn't a silent partner in The Groove and got a say in calling the shots. 'I know you know your way around a bar. Can you stock it? Then check the kegs and the lines?'

'Sure.' Whether Zach knew or not, I wasn't sure, but this was what I had been up to at The Groove these last two weeks. 'I'll let you know if any of them need to be changed.' There was no way I was lifting one of them.

'No worries. Then when you're finished, can you help me set up the stage?'

'Where will the stage be?'

'In the Graphite Beer Garden.' Zach nodded in the direction of the bar that would be used for today's event.

My brother headed off. To where, I didn't know. For the first time in a long time, I was a little unsure of myself. I didn't know where anything was around here, and I knew I would have to ask. But first, I needed to make a list of what I needed. I found a clipboard under the register in the beer garden. I took it to make my list. One side of the page was for Graphite, and the other half was for the Carbon Bar.

An hour later, and with some help from the woman at the concierge desk, the fridges were full and the spirits were stocked. It was time to check the lines and the kegs. I tested the soft drink gun and made sure that was good, too. That took some time, but both bars were good. Time to meet Zach and set up the stage.

When I walked into Graphite, I found the bar was empty of customers, which made it easier for set ups and pull-downs. I didn't notice my brother at first. It wasn't like him to be so lost in thought. He sat on the edge of the black boxes he'd assembled to boost the area he already had set up for small acoustic gigs. I guessed there would be a few people this afternoon, and it would be better if everyone could see who was getting up here to sing.

Zach didn't notice me as I walked in, which I used to my advantage to go straight to the bar and pour the man a drink. I pulled bourbon from the top shelf and poured into a tumbler more than a standard shot's worth over a small amount of ice. I walked over to my brother, two glasses in my hand. Zach's bourbon in one and my water in the other.

'You look like you need a drink.' I handed Zach his bourbon.

He took it, shot it down and let out a cough. The bourbon must have caught on its way down.

'Everything okay?' I didn't know what Zach's reply would be. We weren't that close, but I was here today because he'd asked for my help. I may never be able to make up for every shitty thing that I had ever done. But I'd decided from the moment I rolled into town today that I would never be that person again. No matter how terrible things got, there would always be a reason to be better.

Zach didn't say anything, and I was okay with that. He and I were not at that place where we shared information about our personal lives. After a few moments of silence while I drank my water and Zach crunched on ice cubes, he said, 'Thanks, I think I needed that.' I raised my head and made eye contact with him. 'You didn't pour yourself one?'

'I'm on the job,' I told Zach. 'Plus, it's way too early for a drink on the rocks.' Truth was, I never usually drank before midday.

'Thanks, Connor.' Zach tried for heartfelt but didn't quite get there.

'You're welcome for the chest hairs you'll now grow,' I joked.

'Shut up.'

'It's true, the cough you let out tells me so.'

'Very funny, Connor.' My brother continued with our light-heartedness.

I enjoyed the banter between us, and I wanted to take this moment and say thank you. 'Lex keeping you up to date with how The Groove is doing?' I stopped to look at Zach to gauge his reaction. His expression was blank.

'It's great that The Groove is doing better.' But I could tell Zach was still distracted.

'I just wanted to thank you for the staff you hired. They do a great job. I know you told Lex to pay them above award, and you can tell by the foot traffic how good things are.'

'Connor, I'm just glad you've turned your life around.'

Zach's words echoed in my head.

Before this conversation got any more sentimental, I changed the topic. 'If you would so kindly get off this stage,' I said, 'there's some equipment that needs to be brought out and set up.'

'You know how to do this? Set up a stage?'

I smirked at the questionable look Zach gave me. There were a few things I hid up my sleeves. This was one of them. It felt good to be able to show that I could do this. I owed my brother that much, to pay back a few small favours. He had helped me out more times than I cared to count. This was one where I could make it up to him.

'What do you think I did as a job, little brother, while I navigated a university degree?' My words gave Zach an insight into the life I'd lived in Melbourne that no one really knew about. 'I was an arsehole in order to get shit done, and after a while, it became harder and harder to turn off.'

'Connor.'

But at the shake of my head, Zach stopped. I didn't want his sympathy.

He put his hand on my shoulder and said, 'If you could get the stage set up, I think I might need a few moments.'

Zach's hand dropped from my shoulder and then he was gone. I pulled my phone from my pocket, chose the playlist Morgan had made for me, and got to work on the stage. Being a little rusty, it took me longer than it used to. But I was done in time for the event to start. I tested the microphone, happy at the volume I'd set. All I needed was a stool in case anyone wanted to sit down when they played today. Like me.

As I stood on the stage, I tested the mic one last time. The sound needed to be perfect. I grabbed the guitar that had been put beside the stage, wanting to know if the guitar sounded okay too. I strummed a couple of cords, then put the guitar down. I needed the right mix of guitar sound and volume from the microphone. Both needed to be heard evenly and not have one overpower the other.

With the set-up complete. I thought I had earned the drink I now wanted. When I got closer to the bar, I saw Zach was back. He put the money drawer in the register as I took a seat at the bar. I didn't have to say anything. Zach poured a standard shot of bourbon from the same bottle I used and handed over a glass with no ice. Somehow Zach knew I wouldn't need the ice.

'What about you?' I asked after I shot the bourbon in one go and let out my holy shit breath. That would even grow hairs on my chest.

'I'm on the job. Can't you see I have an event to run?' He jested, seemingly better now than before, more focused. 'And I'm not about to do it drunk.' We both laughed at how messy that would be.

# Black Eye

# Twenty-eight

After the drink Zach handed me, I made my way out to my truck to change out of clothes I'd worked up a sweat in. I grabbed the jeans I'd put in my bag that fit just right and were nothing like the more expensive brand I used to wear. How things had changed since my run-in with Harley James and the night Zach had kicked me out of his bar. It was the night I'd laid eyes on a hazel-eyed brunette who'd stirred up something inside and was always on mind. I had wanted a clean slate since then and to be a better man for Morgan.

As I changed, I caught sight of my new tattoo out the corner of my eye and smiled to myself. My tattoo artist had done a good job of what I'd wanted. I couldn't wait for Morgan to see it. Then I grabbed my new matte black guitar and headed for the front doors of Black's Bar and Grill.

When I walked back through the front doors, I noticed a crowd had started to build for Zach's event. Making my way towards the bar, I wanted one more drink before I had to get up on the stage and sing. I had never performed on my own before. My brother had never asked me to be a guest at one of his events, either. A sign that maybe Zach had started to forgive me after the stunt I'd pulled with Lex at the last event Zach held here.

The bartender put a tumbler with bourbon mixed with cola in front of me. I handed over my card to pay, but the bartender was having none of it. With a shake of his head, I was dismissed. Something I wasn't used to, a drink on the house. I moved farther along the bar and stood out of the way, drink in one hand, guitar in the other.

I took slow sips of my drink as I'd be no good wasted. There was no way I could avoid this event now. Then, my brother was on stage, and today's event was underway. A good crowd had turned out to watch the local talent of Mulwala. Zach sure knew how to draw in a crowd, including young, old and every age in between.

I observed the local talent, saying hello to the people I knew. I watched as Zach performed first, followed by Brock, Shea, Harley and Lex. A few other locals performed before I was called to the stage. I searched around for Morgan, but after talking to Lex, I knew she wasn't here. She wouldn't get to see me sing to her, or so I thought.

'How's everybody doing today?' I asked the crowd when I reached the microphone. They screamed their cheers back at me, and I thought they all must be enjoying the event my brother had put on. That or they were well and truly happy by now that they had a few drinks in them. 'My name is Connor Black. I've been asked to sing a couple of songs today. I hope you like the ones I've picked out.'

I stepped away from the microphone to grab my guitar. Pulling the stool closer to the stand, I sat myself down. I rested my guitar on my knee and pulled the microphone down now that I was seated, tuning the strings of my guitar and playing my songs. Morgan was the reason for the songs I had chosen.

My set list was as followed:

1. 'Put Me in My Place' – Muscadine Bloodline.

2. 'Must've Never Met You' – Luke Combs.

3. 'Dive' – Ed Sheeran.

I was a little rusty, just like I knew I would be, and had told Zach as much. There were a few clumsy cord changes, but I made it through the songs to the end.

'Thank you,' I said at the end of my three-song set. I stood and took a deep breath as the crowd chapped and cheered me off the stage.

The emcee took over the microphone to draw the event and the evening to a close. But the party wasn't over, the emcee told the crowd. They were invited to continue their party in The Carbon Bar, or at Pepper's for dinner. If these partygoers wanted to wind down a little, the Midnight Wine Bar would be opened for a more relaxed environment. And at the end of the night, if there were still people who wanted to party, then Onyx Nightclub would open.

I put my guitar in the stand and turned around to see the crowd exit. Only security remained now. I pulled down the stage that I had set up earlier today. I knew Zach didn't expect me to, but I did it anyway. It would be one less thing he had to worry about, and it didn't take me long. Pack up was always easier. Once everything was stowed away and the height in the stage had been removed, I texted my brother to let him know I was headed out.

*C: Good job on the event. I'm out. Have a good night.*
*Z: Thanks for your help today, it was much appreciated.*
*C: Anytime. I'll see you around.*
*Z: See you around.*

Now that the Graphite Beer Garden was back to what it normally looked like, the customers were allowed back in. I slipped through the crowd as it built up again and found my way out to my truck, with my guitar in my hand. I put my guitar in its case and jumped in the driver's seat.

My tummy grumbled, and I wondered when I had last eaten. I pointed my truck towards the local take away shop on the way to my sister's house and ordered myself a burger.

When I finished my burger and drove into Lex's driveway, I pulled on the parking brake, shut off the engine and locked the truck doors. I unlocked the front door with the key I still had and made my way up the stairs with my overnight bag in my hand.

Opening my bedroom door, I couldn't help but curl my lips upwards at what I saw: Morgan asleep in my bed. Kicking off my boots and stripping down to my black boxer briefs, I crawled into bed next to my woman and kissed the column of her neck the same as she had kissed me.

I pulled Morgan close, wrapped my arm around her and pressed my skin into hers. I felt the tingles deep down from our skin touching. Could she feel how hard I was pressed into the curve of her arse? I was happy to stay like this forever. It felt way too good wrapped up like this.

Man, I had to tell her and soon.

I just had to find the right time to say what needed to be said. Now wasn't that time. I wanted to sleep and to remember the words I told her.

'Connor?' Morgan's words were groggy.

'Umm,' was my non-committal response.

'Tell me this is not a dream? I so badly, want this to not be a dream.'

'I'm right here, Angel.' I kissed Morgan's shoulder this time and felt my skin come alive from the tips of my toes to where my lips pressed into her skin.

Morgan rolled over to face me. 'Lex called me to let me see you sing. I love hearing your voice dedicating songs to me. It makes me feel like an angel.'

# Twenty-nine

I woke out of the deep sleep I was in and felt the bed next to me. Morgan wasn't here. Wasn't curled up in front of me. She had been here though. We'd talked. Even if it was only briefly. I had wrapped my arm around her and held her tight, pressed my skin into hers.

I heard footsteps on the stairs, but knew it wasn't Lex. I had already told her I was staying here. That left Morgan, a sight I thought I'd never see: my Angel here instead of gone. As the door opened, my eyes followed the movement of the door, and I got to see Morgan as she crawled back into bed.

She had gone to get breakfast, and she had come back. I lay there and stared up at her. She was unaware I was now awake. Morgan put two coffees and two brown paper bags down on the bedside table, stripped out of the clothes she'd pulled on, and crawled back under the doona. Then, she leaned against the pillows and the headboard and took a sip of her coffee. She had pulled off surprising me with breakfast better than the time I tried to surprise her and ending up in hospital.

I wanted to take away the coffee she held onto and kiss her until she wanted me inside her. But I didn't pull Morgan down and trap her under me. I leaned in, pressed my nose, then my lips onto the closest bare skin I could reach. Her thigh. My first touch of her skin since my hospital stay. Morgan startled a little and almost spilled her coffee. She rested her coffee back on the bedside table and moved to roll me over and straddle me.

'Jesus, Connor.' That was before I grabbed her and rolled her over so she was trapped underneath me. Okay, I couldn't help myself.

I kissed Morgan just to taste the coffee and caramel on her lips. She tasted so damn good. I wanted more. More kisses that tasted like coffee.

My hand smoothed the hair from her face, and I kissed along her bare shoulder. As my thumb brushed just under her eye, that was when I felt the tiniest roughness along the edge of her eye. My head moved quickly away from the attention I was giving her shoulder to take in the sight of her. My nostrils flared at the small scar I saw. I wanted to get up in this moment to go and kick her brother's arse into next week. But I didn't even get a chance to move off the bed.

Morgan moved one of her hands to my chest and put her other hand on my cheek. She brushed her thumb along my cheekbone. She brought her lips closer to mine, lips that gently pressed into mine, and in that moment all my anger disappeared.

'What happened, Morgan? Lex told me your brother smashed your phone. She didn't, however, tell me he hurt you again.' This was going one of two ways. Either Morgan talked to me, or I rang my sister to ask her what happened. I really hoped Morgan talked to me.

'Now. You want to know what happened? Right now?'

All I could do was nod my head.

'Can we eat first?'

Did Morgan want to avoid talking about this? I didn't want to think so.

I rolled off her and laid flat on my back. Morgan sat up, looked down at me and gave me a sheepish smile. Angel was gorgeous. She knew she had affected me in a way that made me want her right now. But I didn't touch her. I told her we could eat before she told me what had happened. I took a deep breath, sat up, leant back against the headboard on my old bed, and took what Morgan handed me. Coffee and food.

My lips curled upwards at the taste of the coffee. Morgan knew what I liked. I put my coffee down to open the bag. The smell of egg and bacon hit me, and I heard my stomach grumble. Apparently, my stomach already knew this toasted sandwich would be tasty.

Around my first mouthful of food, I managed, 'This is so good.'

'You know your sister-in-law made it. She makes the best toasted sandwiches. Harley's bakery makes lunches for the teachers three days a week.'

I thought maybe I had missed something big in my family. But Morgan spoke as though Harley was already part of the family. My brother just needed to hurry up and ask for that woman's hand and marry her. Zach was out of sorts yesterday. Maybe he needed to work up the courage to ask Harley to be his wife?

I finished my sandwich, took another sip of my still too-hot coffee before I said, because I couldn't help myself, 'What happened, Morgan?'

I could see the tears in her eyes, but they didn't fall. 'I couldn't extend my leave passed your stay in hospital. There were twenty kids that needed their teacher. I don't have the luxury to come and go as I please.' Morgan frowned at me. Tears still pooled in her eyes.

There was a silence between us. Morgan seemed lost in thought as she wiped under her eyes and ate the rest of her toasted sandwich. Same as mine, egg and bacon. Morgan made me wonder if she wasn't sure of what she should say. Just when I thought she wouldn't talk to me, Morgan turned to face me and sat beside me with her legs crossed. I eyed her carefully while she took slow sips of her coffee. Was what I wanted to know too much for Morgan to talk about?

It wasn't.

'My brother found me. I don't know how, but Mulwala is a small town, and everyone knows everyone. Lex and I had gone for dinner, and Jaime wanted to try out his new menu. Lex said she needed a few things from Jackie's office, so I waited by the back bar while she got what she needed.' Morgan stopped to count out a couple of deep breaths.

'I noticed you'd called and was reading your message when Lucas came in and lost his shit. He's so mad at you for knocking him out that he grabbed me and my phone. He tried to drag me out, and I couldn't stop him. I tried to break free, but he wouldn't let me go. I stomped on his foot so damn hard with the heel of my shoe. Lucas smashed my phone as he tried to regain his balance, and pieces of my phone went everywhere. One piece cut under the corner of my eye.'

'I want to kill him,' I told Morgan in an even tone. She had no idea from the moment I covered her mouth with mine that I've wanted to put a protective bubble around her and fight anyone who tried to hurt her, especially her brother.

'I know. But I haven't seen Lucas since that night.' Morgan whispered, then took a moment to finish her coffee. Then, before I could say anything else she said. 'I screamed then, and Lex heard. Connor, you should have seen your sister, she was so badass. She came out of the office and into view so fast that my head spun. Lex growled at my brother and brought him to his knees with her martial arts. I think she might've even broken his wrist. I don't think he will ever hurt me again. He took off then, and your sister even took me to the hospital for the nurse to clean up my eye. Lex called the police too, to tell them Lucas had violated his DVO.'

'The next time he tries to hurt you, I will do more than knock him out,' I stated matter-of-factly.

'Jesus, Connor, you're as bad as Lex,' Morgan replied. 'Lex offered me comfort I never knew I needed that night. Like how siblings should treat each other. She is so easy to talk to. I told her all about Lucas, his temper and the things he's done since he moved in with me. I am grateful of Lex's offer to stay with her. I choose the room we shared together that night, but it only made me miss you even more. Every day since I left you, I wanted to ask Lex if I could borrow her car and drive down to see you. Lucas killed my adventurous spirit over the last twelve months, and I find it hard to step outside my comfort zone now.'

Morgan had lived with the abuse of the brother for twelve months, so it was no wonder she was scared to try new things, like driving down to see me or coming along to last night's event at Zach's bar.

'I'm sorry, Morgan, for the way things have been between us. That my past caught up with me and that your brother came looking for you.' I wanted Morgan to know I would never let anyone hurt her from now on. 'But from this moment until my last breath I will protect you.'

'I know.' Morgan silenced me with her finger on my lips. I reached for her hand that touched my lips and kissed her fingers. 'What happened to calling me Angel?' she asked, her frown returning.

'Not many people call you Morgan, do they?'

With the shake of her head, Morgan had answered me.

'You deserve to be called the name your parents gave you. Not the nickname's others have chosen—myself included.'

'I missed you.' But I was not quick enough to form a reply when I heard this woman say, 'I missed how safe I felt when you're around. I missed the protective bubble you put around me.'

'You missed me?' I still had a hold of Morgan's hand. I pulled her until she had no other choice but to sit on my lap.

Morgan nodded her head as she moved closer to me. When I had Morgan right where I wanted her, I wrapped both of her arms around my neck and moved my hands to the sides of her face. I didn't want Morgan to move when I whispered, 'I missed you, too.'

Morgan's eyes watered again, and it wasn't long before her cheeks were wet and so were my thumbs.

'I missed you, Morgan,' I told her again. 'I missed the feel of you in my arms and the mornings when you were gone. I missed the time we could've spent together and the way you would snuggle up to me. I missed the tender moments we shared, your kisses and the feel of you underneath me. I would be crazy if I missed this moment to tell you that I love you.'

'Connor,' Morgan whispered as she tried to dry her eyes with a wipe of her hands across her face. 'No one has ever said those words to me, and I don't know how love is supposed to feel. But I missed you.'

Silence filled the space around us, then Morgan surprised me with, 'I missed that you weren't here to hold me and the challenge I faced just to wriggle out each time. I missed you and me together in the same bed. I missed your arm wrapped around me at the end of a long day and the way you always made me feel safe. I missed those moments you made me feel like a princess and the way my lips always tingled when you kissed me.'

Morgan's words surprised me as I didn't expect them from her. I wiped her tears away with my thumbs and brought her lips closer to mine. Our lips almost touched when Morgan said, 'If the way you make me feel is how love is meant to feel, then I love you too, baby.'

# Thirty

The words Morgan said unlocked something inside me, and I couldn't help but crash my lips into hers. We kissed for what seemed like a long time, but in reality, it was only until we were both breathless. I wanted Morgan more than I ever thought I would. I wanted to kiss my way all over her skin until I found my way inside her body. But I didn't move a muscle as there was a need to take this moment slowly.

Morgan took her time, too. She straddled me and moved her hands like this was the first time she'd had to discover my body. Her hands roamed my chest and abdomen as she felt the muscles that were more defined since I last time saw her. My rehabilitation required I be physically stronger before the doctor at the hospital signed off on my health and I was allowed to leave Melbourne for good. Morgan's hands moved along my arms, down my chest and over my abs, I knew she liked what she saw, the change in my body. I also knew Morgan liked the feel of my muscles under her hands by the moans that left her mouth.

By the look in Morgan's eyes and the purse of her lips, a little tell, she liked the view of the tattoo that now covered my upper arm and pec muscle, now that my tee-shirt had been removed. Morgan moved closer to me, leaned in to kiss my angel tattoo, and then trailed kisses to the guitar on my left upper arm. Her approval meant the world to me. I couldn't help it then. I moved my hands from her face to under her legs. I picked her up and laid her down gently on the bed that had once belonged to me.

I had to stop Morgan's hands before they travelled any further down my body. She may have wanted to know what the rest of me felt like, but with the way I felt and how much I wanted her this could be over before it had even begun. So, I couldn't help but sink some of my weight into her. She squirmed and let out an excited breath, another moan that made me think she liked that.

Now that Angel was under me, I realised there would be no one else but her and if she ever knew how much she affected me, a case of blue balls would be the least of my worries.

I stared down at Morgan as she stared up at me. I knew she could feel how hard I was pressed into her softness. But unless Morgan told me the words I wanted to hear, nothing more would happen.

'I want you, Connor.'

But I didn't get to open my mouth as then Morgan was busy kissing me. She had reached up peck kisses on my lips.

'Make me feel sexy, just like a princess.' Her next words were a whisper, but I didn't have to make her tell me. 'Connor, I want you to make me come.'

I kissed Morgan until she was breathless once more, then I peeled off her singlet and pulled her shorts down. Both landed in a pile on the floor. I kissed bare skin from the top of Morgan's panties up her body until I reached her bra, which I peeled off her body, too. I could see Morgan had been to see Shea for more clothes, similar to the ones I had bought her.

I bypassed the attention her breasts deserved to kiss up to her neck, along her jaw and down along her shoulder. Morgan shuddered with every one of my kisses that landed on her body. My stubble must have made her body shiver. For every kiss I gave I felt the electricity travel through me, and I wondered if Morgan felt the same electricity I did.

Morgan's shudders turned to squirms the more my kisses landed on lightly tanned skin, and I wondered how worked up I had made her. When her hands landed on either side of my face, I sensed she wanted to have her way with me, that and she needed a moment to catch her breath. I rolled us over. I was now at her mercy.

Morgan kissed me the same way I just kissed her, and I now knew why she needed a break. I didn't know how much longer I could play and not be inside her. My hands grabbed Morgan's when I felt her reach for the band of my briefs. Was she ready for this? For the way this would feel. For me?

'Morgan.' My hands wrapped around hers, and I couldn't move her head to look at me. 'Morgan,' I repeated, but she still didn't look at me. 'Angel,' I whispered, and when her eyes met mine. 'I don't have any protection.'

'Baby.' Morgan's eyes stayed glued to mine. 'I'm on the pill. I talked to the nurse at the hospital after she patched up my eye.' Morgan's words ended on a whisper.

'Bare?' I asked. 'Are you sure?' *Were we both ready for this?* ran on a loop in my head.

'I am aware of the risks,' Morgan told me softly before she kissed me. 'I'm not scared anymore. I know you love me, Connor.'

I let go of Morgan's hands and let her peel my briefs down over my painfully hard cock and off my legs. At the end of the bed, Morgan stripped out of the last of her clothes, naked, beautiful and mine. Morgan took a step back towards the bed, then she knelt and moved closer to me. She straddled me, and I couldn't help but reach up, cup her face, and let my fingers tangle in her hair.

Morgan straightened me up and ran the head of my cock through the wetness of her pussy. She lined me up, then slowly lowered herself onto me. When every inch of me was inside her, I felt my cock pulsate. I took a deep breath. No way was this about to last long. My thumb stroked over Morgan's cheek as I brought her lips closer to mine. I kissed her and let my tongue dance with hers. I hoped she was ready for this.

Our hips moved apart, then together. We fell into a rhythm. I would pulsate, and she would tighten around me. I knew it was only a matter of time before we were both on the edge of bliss. But I told Morgan she would always come first, so I let my thumb find its way over Morgan's skin to the lips of her pussy to rub steady circles over her clit.

I knew she was close to the edge and about to fall off when she breathed my name. As soon as I felt Morgan tighten around me, I was done for. I felt my body harden, a sign I was close. One more pump of my hips and I released my seed inside of her.

I filled Morgan just like I knew I would have the last time we had sex. But unlike last time, I wasn't in a hurry to pull out of her. Our hips slowed in their movements now that we had reached our climax and fallen into the abyss. Morgan stared down between her legs she must already see what leaked out.

I picked her up and rolled us over, falling out of her when I laid her down. I kissed her forehead and went in search of a warm washcloth. In the bathroom, I found what I needed and warmed it under the tap before taking it back to Morgan. Curled in a ball, Morgan's eyes had drifted closed. I put the warm cloth between her legs and let the warmness to soothe her sensitive skin.

I kissed her temple, but I needed a shower and to clean myself up. With my bag in tow I headed for the bathroom.

The hot water steamed the bathroom, and I let the shower spray massage my back. I had zoned out. I was a little lost in thought knowing I still had to tell Morgan about what I had done while we were apart. I didn't hear the shower door open or close. Morgan's arms travelled up my back and down my arms, she kissed my shoulder then wrapped her arms around me.

'You look good, baby. Your bruises are gone.' I turned around to face her.

'The doctors made me pass a physical before I could leave Melbourne.'

Morgan only giggled at me as she shook her head. She didn't believe me.

I pulled my woman closer to my body. 'I also took self-defence lessons. The exercise regime is brutal.'

'The ones your mother organised.' At my raised eyebrow Morgan quickly continued, 'I overheard the conversation your mother had with your father.'

'Yes,' was the simple reply I gave her.

'I like your muscles and the story of your tattoo. It suits you,' Morgan whispered before she leaned her head on my shoulder.

'I'm glad you like it.' Then before I lost my nerve, I blurted out. 'Come for a drive with me.'

Morgan raised her eyebrow back at me, curious as to what I was up to. 'Okay,' she told me warily.

Morgan watched me while I lathered shower gel and rinsed it off. I kissed her, and I wanted her again already. But if I wanted to show her what I had recently acquired, we would have to leave before I started anything new.

'Jesus, Connor, I want you again already.'

'I want you too.'

Morgan shivered when I whispered in her ear.

'But if we don't leave now, we will never leave.'

'I'm okay with that,' Morgan told me with a sexy, wicked smirk on her face.

That almost undid me and had me pushing her up against the wall of the shower to have my way with her. 'I will keep that in mind.' I stepped out of the shower.

I left Morgan to cleanse while I dried off and got dressed. My woman found me in my room at the end of the bed, and I pulled on my boots and looked up to see her beautiful body naked in front of me.

I wanted to reach out and touch her, but Morgan stayed just out of reach. She didn't shy away from me as she dressed her-self. The clothes she chose were the ones I'd purchased for her, the tee-shirt dress that hugged her figure. Morgan pulled on her Sketchers and grabbed the flannelette shirt I'd also brought her, before she moved closer, straddled my hips and leaned into nibble on my lip.

'I'm ready,' she taunted me. 'We can go now.'

I stood up and held her to my body, then I let her slide down me. 'You will pay for that,' I taunted back. Morgan's body trembled. Did she like the feel of the muscle she held onto, or was it the thought of what might happen later?

# Thirty-one

'Connor.' Morgan turned to face me. We had only gone two kilometres down the road. 'You can't be here, you know this.'

'Morgan.' I met her stare. 'I'm not here to cause trouble. I have to hand in my keys and grab the things I left behind. I haven't had a chance to do that yet.'

My truck was parked in the carpark of The Grand Hotel. I got out, the keys to the pub in one hand and my truck keys in the other. I pocketed my keys as Morgan followed me.

Unsure of what would happen when I entered the pub, I opened the door of the front bar and let Morgan stride in before me. Heads turned to watch me as I walked up to the bar. It had been a couple of months since I had been here. Were the patrons surprised to see me? Did they wonder why I hadn't been behind the bar? Why the bar had been closed and only recently reopened when Jackie, Jarryd and Jason had gotten back from Melbourne.

'The bar looks good, Jaime.' The man behind the bar was tired, a sign that I knew he had been working a lot of hours.

'Thanks to Brock for the repairs and to you and Alex. You have all gotten us back on track.' Jackie would never have spilled that truth unless she had told Lex, who in turn told Jaime. I knew Jackie kept matters of her business close to her chest, and I just hoped now she would let Lex continue to help her.

'I'm glad everything is going well. Keep up the good work, man.' I couldn't help but encourage the man to keep on keeping on.

I knew it wouldn't be long before Jackie came out to check on things around the pub. That was how she did things.

'Connor.' She was surprised to see me standing next to Morgan in the front bar, because the last time she saw me, I had been in Melbourne. Our paths had crossed as outpatients attending physio appointments at St Vincents Hospital. Jackie's surgery had been successful, and she was steadily recovering five weeks later.

'I'm not here to cause trouble.' With my hands up, my pub keys hung from my fingers. 'I just want to grab my things and leave the keys.'

Jackie didn't say anything, just moved her head towards the stairs, the go-ahead I needed to get my things. Morgan followed me. I was only upstairs for a few minutes. That was how long it took to pile everything I had left behind into the backpack I had also left here. I took one last look around. There was nothing I had forgotten. Morgan entwined her fingers with mine. This was where it all started for us. The moment was surreal, and I felt sentimental leaving the pub behind. At the bottom of the stairs, I checked my locker for anything that may be in there. There was nothing.

I knocked on Jackie's door, the pub keys in one hand and Morgan still holding the other. Jackie looked up at me as I stood, like I always did, at the threshold to her office.

'Here are your keys.' I stepped up to Jackie's desk to put them on top.

'Connor!' The way Jackie said my name, I couldn't help but stand back and give her my full attention. 'I may have been a little harsh on you at the hospital when I let you go.' Jackie took a deep breath. 'I'm sorry.'

I opened my mouth to say something, but nothing came out, so I closed it again. Jackie continued like I wasn't about to interrupt.

'If it wasn't for you and Alex, I would have had to close the pub for good.'

Jackie's words caught me off guard. I wasn't aware the things I did helped all that much. Maybe I was wrong. Maybe paying the bills stopped the wheels from falling off. I guess I would never know unless I asked Lex.

'I need someone like you in my corner, Connor.'

I was slightly confused by this conversation. It was a one-eighty from when Jackie was laid up in her hospital bed.

'Your sister cleaned up my office mess. She is one incredible woman. But I need someone to pay the bills when I can't. I need someone to kick out rowdy customers and pick me up off floor. I need my sons to get off my back because I didn't see all these good things happening around me. I need you, Connor. I need you to help me with this pub so we can all have a break.'

'I don't know what to say.' I didn't expect my day to go this way. I was a little blown away.

'The job is yours if you want it. Tell me you will at least think about it.' An offer of a job. A job I wanted to do. A job I knew I would eventually have to look for.

'Let me think about it, and I'll let you know.' I couldn't make any promises. If there was one thing the woman next to me had taught me, it was that promises could be broken, and I didn't want to promise anything to anyone.

'Connor.' The sound of my name halted me from leaving. 'You may not have been there in the hospital every day when my boys came to visit. But every day they came in so excited, Jason and Jarryd gave me a running commentary about what the three of you had been up to. You run a tight ship at The Groove Jarryd tells me. I know where you learned those skills. Please tell me you will seriously think about my offer?'

'Thanks to Zach hiring decent staff, it's easier to run a tight ship. He's my younger brother and I'm the one looking up to him. I'm in awe of his business savvy,' I confessed.

'Connor, I have seen the way you work. I know you used what you learned under my wing to do what you do at The Groove.'

I gave a heartfelt smile. Jackie was right. I took what I'd learnt at The Grand to help me at The Groove. My hard work was noticed. It was nice to be appreciated. 'Let me think about your offer.' Though my gut instinct told me I would be crazy to not seriously consider Jackie's offer. But I had to talk to Morgan first. Working at The Grand wouldn't happen unless Angel approved.

Morgan and I waved goodbye as we made our exit out the way we come in.

'Wow.' I opened the door to my truck and got in.

'You could have your job back if you want it.' There was a knowing smile on Morgan's face that told me it wouldn't be a bad thing if all I did was work behind a bar.

'The nights wouldn't bother you?' I needed to know that Morgan would be okay if I accepted Jackie's job offer and spent my nights working and not with her.

Morgan shook her head as I started my truck.

'You think I should take Jackie up on her offer?' I asked, wondering why Morgan would want that for me.

'You will be miserable if you don't.' My woman had a point.

What else would I do with my time? Even with the bills I'd paid at The Grand and The Groove, the house I'd bought that still needed to be renovated, and the truck that I had just purchased, there was still plenty of money left. Even with the added bills of my Melbourne apartment. Now that The Groove had started to turn a healthy profit again, I didn't really need to work. But Morgan was right. I would be bored as soon as the house was renovated.

'Is that right?' I reversed out of the pub carpark and headed towards the place I wanted to show Morgan.

'After the novelty of not having a job wears off, you'll wish you had one to go to.'

'I've got a project that will keep me busy for a little while, but you're right once the novelty wears off. I'll probably drive us both crazy.'

'What project, Connor? What did you do?' Morgan tried to raise one eyebrow at me but didn't quite pull it off.

'Let me just show you.'

When Morgan told me okay, there was a hint of uncertainty in her voice. I guess I would just have to show my angel how she deserved to be treated, because she deserved the world.

Morgan and I exchanged glances before she continued to look out the windscreen, realisation dawning on her face as she noticed where we were headed.

'Connor, this is private property. There's nothing up here but the water tower. You need to turn around.' Morgan reached out and grabbed my arm. Something told me she didn't want to come up here. Then I heard her whisper. 'Please turn around. Please take me back to Lex's.'

I stopped my truck in the middle of the bitumen road. I turned to look at the women beside me. 'Morgan.' But she wouldn't look at me. 'Angel,' I whispered to get her attention. 'Talk to me?'

'Nothing good happens up here.' Morgan said through her sniffle, and I wondered what she was talking about. Then she continued. 'Scott, my brother's friend, was meant to take me to Lucas, not somewhere he could force himself on me.'

There were a few moments' silence, and then through her silence, Morgan recalled what happened that night.

'He had me up against the boot of his car, but he wasn't ready. When the idiot let go of me to undo his buckle, I pushed so hard he fell hard on his arse and that's when I made a move for the driver's seat. I got in, locked the doors, took off and left him there.'

The emotion in Morgan's voice stunned me as I sat there and listened. 'After my brother left me battered on the floor, he threatened he would leave me up here, the same way I'd left Scott.' Morgan was silent, then on whispered words, I heard, 'So no, I don't want to be up here.'

'Do you trust me?' I cupped Morgan's face with the hand that wasn't on the steering wheel. Morgan leaned her head into my touch, and her head turned my way. Her eyebrow was raised, and that told that me in this minute she wasn't sure if she should trust me. I didn't say anything to reassure her. I just continued to drive us up the road towards the water tower.

Our destination wasn't the water tower though. There was a road more than halfway up that I wanted to take Morgan down. I turned off Water Tower Road and onto the dirt road that would lead us to the rundown homestead that was up here. I pulled my truck up in front of the double garage attached to the homestead and got out. Morgan got out at the same time as me, and I had to be quick to round my truck and grab her before she took off out of curiosity.

'I never knew this place was here, and I have lived here for the last two years.'

I had pushed her into the side of my truck and lifted her chin to leave a chaste kiss on her lips because I wanted her to think about me and not the story she had just told me.

'It's a little run-down, but once it's all fixed up, it will be beautiful here,' I whispered, pushing my fingers through her gorgeous hair that she had left out today and leaving more soft kisses on her lips. 'Let me show you around.'

'Wait.'

I turned to head towards the homestead, but she let go of my hand when she didn't come with me.

'All this is yours?' Morgan asked of the homestead and all the property that surrounded the house.

'All this is ours.' I turned back to stand in front of Morgan. She had a shocked look on her face.

'Ours,' Morgan whispered.

I didn't verbally answer Morgan, I just nodded my head. Then I felt her hands wrap around me. On her tippy toes, she reached up to kiss my lips.

'I like the sound of that.' Her face lit up with the biggest smile, and a few happy tears falling down her cheeks.

I showed Morgan around, though there wasn't much to see. The bricks that made up this homestead were in good condition. The front veranda that looked down over the river needed more than a few wooden planks replaced. The roof needed minor repairs and the gutters all needed to be replaced. The whole inside of the house would need gutting. Once the inside was done, our overgrown courtyard and garden would really need my attention. Then I could think about the pool I would like to surprise Morgan with.

I had memorised the report Brock had sent me on the work that needed to be done on the homestead and that was after the bungalow was ready to live in. I didn't tell Morgan any of that, though, as she didn't need to worry. I was going to handle all the renovations. Morgan could sit back, relax, and watch the transformation.

I led Morgan back around to the three-bay carport. There was one more place I wanted to show her. She didn't question me, just followed beside me. I walked past the U-Haul trailer and up the three steps of the bungalow's veranda that was hidden behind the carport.

'It's not much at the moment.' I unlocked and pushed open the door for Morgan to see. She walked past to take a look around inside this empty shell.

'Connor.' Morgan turned in a full circle with an expression on her face that I couldn't quite read.

'Work starts in here tomorrow to make this space liveable while the homestead is renovated.' My words left Morgan a little shell-shocked. 'Until the bungalow is ready, we can continue stay at Lex's.'

Morgan had gone silent as she stared out what would be the lounge room window. I stood behind her and wrapped my arms around her.

'Talk to me?' I wanted to know what she wasn't so sure of.

'You want to do this? With me? We don't even know each other.' It wasn't hard to hear the emotion in her voice again.

'Maybe we don't know each other, but I want to get to know you. If we don't work out, you will never have to live with your brother again. Me, on the other hand, will most likely have to live with Lex again. But don't worry about it. Please just say you will move in with me.'

'Will you always love me? Just like this, reel me back in when I push you away?' Morgan turned around in my arms. 'I need to know you will hold on even if I let go.'

'I will love you with everything I've got. I will never let you go.' I kissed the tip of Morgan's nose. 'Will you always love me and tell me when I'm being a stubborn arse? Will you always pull me closer to you even when I'm pushing you away?'

Morgan nodded in agreement, a wayward grin on her face. 'Baby, you are stuck with me.' Then Morgan whispered, and I shivered. 'I'll move in with you, but you have to take the job Jackie offered.'

'Deal.' I planted my lips on Morgan's and kissed her breathless. Morgan knew, without a doubt, that I would take the job Jackie offered.

# Epilogue

*Three months later*

Our bungalow was finally ready, and I couldn't wait to move in. After three months of little sleep and a lot of blood, sweat and tears, the bungalow was no longer an empty shell. Morgan didn't know that in the process of getting the bungalow ready, I managed to pack all the items that were hers from the place she'd lived with her brother. She hadn't left much behind the day she'd packed what she could, the day we headed to Melbourne. What was left behind was now at the bungalow.

From the day we'd told each other 'I love you', not once did Morgan sneak out. I was ecstatic she would never have to go back to live with her brother. If I wanted Morgan and I to have our own space, I needed to hurry up and move us out of my sister's.

The bungalow was now fully furnished with what I had packed into the U-Haul trailer from my storage unit. Tonight, I would carry Morgan over the threshold of the bungalow's front door, through all the furniture I'd set up, to the only place I wanted us to be: our bed.

When the time came, Morgan could take all of my money and shop for all the furniture for our homestead, but that still needed to be renovated. There were a few things I left in my apartment in Melbourne to make it more homely. Everything else I brought with me. I unpacked only what I needed to make our little home feel comfortable. There was a cosy and homely atmosphere about our bungalow now. What I didn't need to unpack was tucked in on one side of my double garage. I unpacked all of Morgan's things, too. She was right, she didn't have much. But it didn't matter. What was mine was now hers, and I would give her the best when the homestead was ready to be furnished.

But to be able to have the best, I first needed to work my shift at The Grand Hotel. Of course, the only night I didn't want to close was the one night I just wanted to be here with my woman so we could celebrate moving in.

I locked the bungalow door and threw my guitar in the back of my truck. You never knew when a slow night at the pub would come around or when Jackie's teenage sons would challenge me for a jam. Even Jaime had joined in on our jam sessions of late. Now that my recording studio was ready, I had been able to learn a few new songs, a couple I thought I might even like to record for myself.

I pulled into my spot behind The Grand and got out. When Jackie had offered me my old job back, I was surprised when she'd asked if I would like to be her business partner. After

Morgan insisted I take Jackie up on her job offer and Lex's lawyer boyfriend, Brad, looked over the contract, I couldn't say no. When Jackie told her sons about her decision to include me as her partner, they were more excited about the news than either Jackie or I were. It felt good to know that someone liked having me around.

'Connor,' Jackie called from her behind her desk when I walked past.

I backtracked and stood in the office doorway.

'I understand now why you're so fond of this pub, as you remember how family-orientated we were.' Jackie got straight to the point. 'Your parents used to come here all the time. At first by themselves, then with their three young children, Connor, Zach and Alex.' Jackie stopped for a breath. 'It's been a long time since this establishment has had that family-friendly vibe. When I fired you, I thought you were going to chew me up and spit me out that I didn't see you were trying to bring that vibe back. I want to say thank you for everything you've done, and I'm grateful this pub means a great deal to you. You brought Jaime back home, especially when you didn't have to. Even when I fired you, you continued to hold us together.'

Jackie blew me away with the sentimental words she threw my way. I knew Jackie had spoken with Zach and Alex as that was the only way she would know the details of why this pub was special. So, I did the only thing I'd learned how to do, even the score, kindly, and not as the prick I once was. I couldn't help but throw my own sentimental words back at her. 'Jackie.' I needed to get her attention. 'You did what you had to do. When you fired me, I realised I had a long way to go before I would be seen as anything but ruthless. I'm the one that needs to thank you. You took a chance on me when I told you about my fresh start. I will forever appreciate the opportunity you gave me.'

'Well, you're welcome,' Jackie said, sharing a genuine smile with me. 'Now off you go. There's work to be done.'

I nodded and moved away from the doorway. It was good to see Jackie be her normal bossy self as she sat behind her desk and recovered from her heart surgery.

I put my things in my locker and grabbed a tea towel to tuck into the back of my jeans. Now, I was ready to start work. I made my way round the pub, checking both bars and making sure no one needed to be served. When I saw Jarryd had it covered, I made my way to the dining area where Jason was bringing out meals from the kitchen. Jaime had the bistro under control.

'It's slow tonight.' Jason approached me a little later at the back bar. I was about an hour into my shift.

'Yeah, seems that way.' I was cautious as to what Jason had planned. When it was slow, like tonight, he liked to get into mischief.

'Maybe we can jam tonight?' With just one look at Jason, I could tell he was up to something, and I was on to him.

'What are you up to?' I stopped myself just in time from tapping my foot.

'Nothing!' Jason was adamant he wasn't up for causing trouble.

'Spill it, Jason.'

'We haven't sat down to jam just you and me since you've been back.'

Jason was right. He had asked me many times to sit down with him and jam. Most quiet nights, Jaime and Jarryd also joined in.

'Jason.'

'Please, Connor, can we jam tonight. Can we just go and get our guitars?' Jason's look was anything but innocent. 'You did bring your guitar, didn't you?'

'You know I always carry my old beat-up guitar with me.' Jason knew this. 'If your mum says yes, I will get my guitar from the backseat of my truck,' I told Jason and wondered if he would actually go and ask his mother.

When Jason ran off, I assumed he had gone to find his mother, but when he returned with his guitar in hand, I couldn't help but raise my eyebrow.

'Mum said yes.' But I doubted that.

Something told me that I just walked straight into whatever Jason was up to, but somehow it didn't stop me. I still went and got my guitar from my truck. I part-owned this pub now, too, so I could play my guitar if I wanted to.

Jason had set up two chairs in the back bar of the pub, the spot we liked to jam in. When he saw me, Jason took his seat and waited patiently for me to take mine.

'What do you want to play?' I waited for Jason to reply.

'I know your studio is set up, and I want to hear what you have been working on.'

My studio. Now I knew what tonight was all about. Jason wanted to know what song I was working on. Maybe Jason wanted me to invite him to sing in my studio. It was ready, and every chance I had, I practised. It helped me with my clumsy chord changes and to sharpen my skills to want to put together a playlist to play one day, maybe at this pub. Or for one of Zach's events. Whatever was next to eventuate, I would even show up Lex just like old times.

I wasn't sure how Jason knew about my plan, but maybe he overheard my talks with Jackie. If Jason thought tonight was the start of live music in the pub, I had news for him. And if he thought he could spring a jam session on me then I was going to have to make a deal with Jason that he had to show up with the goods too and play me a song – similar to how Lex and I would always try to be better than the other.

'There is one song I've learnt that I'd be happy to play for you,' I told Jason, then waited for him to look at me. 'But first you have to play what you have been working on.'

Jason gave me a look that said he wasn't ready to be in the spotlight.

*Well, bad luck you started this, and I know just how to fin-ish it.* 'Fair's fair.'

Jason strummed his guitar. 'My mum loves this song,' was all he said before he played his rendition of Keith Whitley's 'When You Say Nothing at All'. And I had to give Jason credit. He did a fine job. A lot of practice had gone into the song. When I saw Jackie had made her way out of her office with no expression on her face, I couldn't tell if she had said yes or not. Jackie hadn't put a stop to us yet, so this little show of Jason's went on.

Jason finished his song, and we heard a few claps. He seemed to have attracted an audience for me to play, too. There was no time like the present to take the bull by the horns and play. I looked at the people who had gathered around to see if the one person I wanted to hear this song was in the crowd, but I couldn't see her. I didn't know where she was. I hadn't seen her since she'd left for work this morning.

I tuned the strings of my guitar to how I liked it, then light-ly picked the strings of my guitar. It sat on my knee. I was ready. The song I was about to play started differently than how I planned to play it tonight. 'Dear today...' I sang and let the rest of the lyrics by Luke Combs flow out of me. The first verse I sang was acapella. Then as I got to the chorus, I played my guitar. I built the song through the second verse right to the end where there were even more people gathered around to hear me sing. When I finished, I heard the cheers of many.

'Thank you,' I said to everyone that clapped. I stood and made my exit. Time to put my guitar away and do the work that I actually got paid for. I headed for the back door, lost in thought. I didn't realise until I was almost at my truck that someone had followed me.

I put my guitar on the back seat then turned around at the sound of my name. But Morgan wasn't the person that stole my attention first. That would be my dad. Morgan didn't hesitate to wrap her arms around me when she reached me. She squeezed me tightly as I cupped her face and kissed the tip of her nose.

'Morgan.' I un-cupped her face. 'You remember my dad from the hospital.' Morgan turned her head to look behind her. She let go of me and turned around to face Preston Black.

'Mr Black.' Morgan's voice was a little wobbly, so I grabbed her hand and entwined our fingers.

'Ms Campbell.'

'Dad, what brings you to town?' I knew the man was always busy. Unfortunately, it was the nature of the beast in the line of business he worked in—law enforcement.

'Your mother.' The next words out of his mouth had me hold Morgan's hand a little tighter. 'Your mother wanted to make the trip up from Melbourne to tell you in person that I caught the bastard who put you in the hospital. The same idiot who roughed up your sister.'

I now vaguely remembered that conversation from my first day in hospital. My dad had pieced together from the statements both Alex and I had made that Paul had tried to use Lex to get to me and my money. But if I knew my dad, Paul was in a hole so deep and so dark he wouldn't see daylight again. Of all the times my dad had bailed me out for the shit I'd done, he would never have been able to get me off a murder charge.

'Thank you,' came out once I had comprehended what my dad had just told me.

'As for your brother, Morgan.' My dad gave her his full attention. 'My colleagues inform me he has been detained for the mess he made here at the pub, his assault on you and the little side business he thought he could get away with. If he's not careful, he will end up in the same hole as the arsehole who touched my son and daughter.'

Morgan and I both looked at each other. But my dad hadn't finished, so we turned our attention back to him.

'Morgan, your brother won't be back, as he has violated his restraining order. As for the house, Lucas will have to pay for the interior damage and the broken furniture. Your brother hid money in his mattress. Once the damages have been paid, I will see to it that you get what is left, okay, Morgan.'

'Thank you,' we said in unison. Morgan had said her brother had been absent of late, and I wondered if the Mulwala police had been the reason why.

'Come and have a drink with your old man,' my dad said, sticking his hand out for me to shake.

'Maybe next time you're in town?' I hoped my dad got my drift that I just wanted to take Morgan home.

I guess he did understand because after he shook my hand, he smirked with one eyebrow raised. Before he went on his merry way back inside the pub, he had me pondering if he was considering retirement. 'Next time I'm in town you won't be able to get rid of me so easily.'

'Wow,' Morgan said under her breath, and it wasn't hard to hear the amazement in her voice. 'Your dad is incredible. He followed up to find out my brother's being detained. How much money do you think was stashed in the mattress?'

'Enough to make you happy.' I turned Angel so we faced each other. I reached out to rub my thumb over her neck and shoulder before I whispered. 'I will never let anyone hurt you, Morgan. Ever.'

'I know, baby,' Morgan whispered back as she moved closer to me.

I couldn't help but smash my lips onto hers and kiss her like she belonged to me. 'Time to go.' I traced my fingers down Morgan's shoulder to her fingers to hold her hand. I moved closer to my truck, but Morgan didn't follow me.

'What about your shift?' Morgan asked of the hours I still had left to work.

'Jaime can cover it.' I pulled my phone out to text Jaime.

'Connor.' She wanted to let go of my hand, but I wouldn't let her. She was hesitant. I didn't know why she didn't want to leave.

'Angel.' I stepped away from my truck and closer to her. When I was close enough, I whispered. 'All I want to do is lay you down and make love to you.' I took a deep breath and let my words sink in. 'I can't do that if you don't come with me, and we are not going to my sister's to do what I want to do to you.'

'Oh.' But there was still something on her mind. This time when I pulled on Morgan's hand, she followed me.

The cab of my truck was quiet as I drove towards the water tower. Both of us were lost in thought as I pulled into our driveway. When I parked in the carport, Morgan turned to look at me.

'Connor?' Morgan questioned me as she reached for the door handle. I wondered if I answered her that I would still be quick enough to catch her before she got out of my truck.

'Morgan,' I whispered. 'The bungalow is ready.'

I rounded my truck to open her door.

I stepped closer to her and softly kissed her lips. 'Come on, I want to show you around,' I told her, but really all I wanted to do was lay Morgan down on our bed.

Morgan's hand covered her mouth in shock as I picked her up. Her legs automatically wrapped around my waist. She held onto me as I held onto her. With my arms around Morgan's waist, I carried her up the three steps to the bungalow, over the threshold of the front door. Morgan twisted and turned in my arms. But I didn't stop. I didn't let her go as I made my way through the open-plan living of our bungalow. Morgan could check everything out later, after I had made love to her.

'Connor.' Morgan put her hands on either side of my face to make sure she had my full attention. 'Where did all this furniture come from?'

'Surprise,' was all that I could say to my woman. I didn't tell her where I'd got all the furniture. I just continued to walk us towards our bed.

'Connor,' rushed out of Morgan as I dropped her onto the bed. Morgan squirmed on the doona cover as she took in how this room was styled. Dark grey and soft pink.

I covered Morgan with my body and whispered in her ear, 'If you don't like it, you can change it. You can decorate it however you want.'

But Morgan didn't ask how or with what money. No, Morgan asked, 'Would you really put a diamond on my hand?' The lyrics from the song I had sung tonight.

I nodded towards the box on the bedside table, the one she hadn't seen yet. Morgan looked over her shoulder to see what I had put there. There was a black velvet box with a white gold princess-cut diamond ring inside, just for her.

'Oh, thank God.' Morgan was breathless, and I knew this was why she was hesitant outside the pub and quiet on the way home.

'Angel, talk to me?' I kissed along her jaw.

'I always thought I would be married when I had children.' I stopped kissing her.

'Baby?' I was a little shocked. The word fell from my mouth as I took a minute to comprehend that I had gotten my woman pregnant.

'Yes. You, me and a baby makes three.' Morgan's words were barely a whisper as she tried to read my reaction.

'What about your contraception?' I was distracted with thoughts that ran through my head. Was I ready to be a dad?

'Apparently you have super swimmers.' Morgan took my face in her hands and kissed me. She knew my mind was elsewhere. I was blown away.

'Connor, baby.' I stopped her next words with my finger on her lips. I had plenty of time to get ready to be a dad, like the rest of my woman's pregnancy. Right now, Angel needed me. She wanted to know if I was okay with her baby news. So, I shocked her.

'Marry me?' I whispered into her ear and started to kiss along her jaw again. I felt Morgan shiver under me.

'Make love to me,' Morgan replied, and I slowly undressed the woman underneath me.

I stood to strip out of the clothes I wore then I covered Morgan with my nakedness and kissed her deeper than I had ever kissed anyone before. I didn't check to see if she was ready for me, I just sank all of myself inside her. Morgan gasped. I guessed she really wasn't ready for me.

'I love you,' fell out of my mouth at the end of our kiss. I wouldn't move until she talked to me.

Morgan whispered, 'Yes,' and I knew that was the answer to my question about marriage. 'I love you, baby.'

Those words did something to me every time I heard Morgan say them. When she reached up to kiss me, I knew I needed to move and make love to the woman that would be my wife—the mother of my child. I had my work cut out for me now, to get the homestead ready for my family. I was a changed man, and a better man all for it. My slate was finally clean.

# ACKNOWLEDGEMENTS

Thank you to my editor and publisher Juliette Lachemeier at The Erudite Pen, who inspired the honing of my writing craft. I know the edges of book two aren't as rough. To my book cover designer Judith San Nicolas for taking the ideas I have thrown into the mixing pot to come out with a totally drool-worthy cover – your work is amazing. To my wonderful family and husband Craig – you are still encouraging me to pursue my writing dreams. To my mum Susan for being my sounding board and the person who reads the messy first drafts. To Tegan, Kerrie, Cheryl, Rhonda and Tallaya for being brave enough to read the words I have written. Your insight is invaluable and your support is truly appreciated as I work on making The Acoustic Make You Mine Romance Series a reality.

# ABOUT THE AUTHOR

Kimberley Anne was born and raised on the border of New South Wales and Victoria. The small country town she grew up in is the inspiration for the fictional town in her novel. Kimberley completed her Bachelor of Arts in 2001 where she majored Professional Writing at Victoria University, Melbourne. She began writing her debut novel in 2018 after her husband gifted her a Kindle.

With life experience on her side, Kimberley moved on from her country-town beginnings and is now based in Brisbane, Australia. When Kimberley isn't looking for her next book idea or having her nose in her Kindle, she can be found kicking back with a margarita in her hand and her German Shepherds at her feet.

*Black Eye* is Kimberley's second book in the Make You Mine Romance novels, Acoustic Series, where she blends romance with real-life challenges, music, passion and plenty of heat. Her debut novel *Blackout*, the first book in the series, was met with rave reviews and flew off the shelves.

Enjoyed the book? You can follow the author at:


Website: www.kimberleyanneauthor.com

Email: info@kimberleyanneauthor.com

FB: https://www.facebook.com/authorkimberleyanne

Instagram: www.instagram.com/kimberleyanneauthor/

If you liked the book, please leave a review on Amazon, Goodreads or with the author directly. Reviews are invaluable in supporting an author's hard work and are greatly appreciated.